An Unorthodox Romance

a novel

An Unorthodox Romance

a novel by

Brenda Barrie

GRAY MATTER IMPRINT EDITION

Library of Congress Cataloging-in-Publication Data
Barrie, Brenda
An Unorthodox Romance, a novel / Brenda Barrie
    Fiction, Novel,
    ISBN 978-0-9835921-8-1 (978-0-9835921-9-8 Kindle version)
    ISBN 0983592187
    ISBN 13 9780983592181
    1. Novel. 2. Fiction. 3. Jewish Marriage. 4. Israeli Marriage. 5. Romance.
6. Women Rabbis. 7. Egalitarian Judaism. 8. Orthodox Judaism

    Artwork used for the cover of *An Unorthodox Romance* is a detail from an original piece entitled *The Chuppah* by Irina Ruth Rabinikov. Cover design and typesetting is by Rena Konheim, RBSafran Design.

Published by Gray Matter Imprints™, division of *Gray Matter Consultants LLC*, P.O. Box 50278 Irvine, CA 92619

10 9 8 7 6 5 4 3 2 1

Printed in the United States of America by

    Gray Matter accepts queries only.at:
    Gray Matter Imprints
    P.O. Box 50278
    Irvine, CA 92619

Publisher's Note: This novel is a work of fiction. The names, characters, organizations, places and incidents are either the product of the author's imagination or, as in the case of Israel and Los Angeles, are used fictitiously, and any resemblance to actual persons (living or dead), events or locales is entirely coincidental.

Praise for

AN UNORTHODOX ROMANCE

What happens at the intersection of ambition and obligation? And which do we trust: The heart or our intellect? With An Unorthodox Romance, Brenda Barrie continues her fearless and compassionate exploration of the lives of people of faith. Marnie Holland immediately earns her place alongside Tovah Feldner and Barrie's other amazing and always believable characters; individuals who manage their way through the complications of life, using all that has been given them and nothing more powerful than their decency and their truth. This memorable page-turner will linger in your imagination for a long, long time.

- **David Haynes**, author of *A Star In The Face Of The Sky*

Brenda Barrie's latest book takes you into the world of Rabbi Marnie Holland, a Reform rabbi teaching at the modern University of Judaism in the 1990s, but also teaching at a very traditional Yeshiva, both in L.A.

In addition to straddling the many communal lines in Judaism, *An Unorthodox Romance* includes a duplicitous ex-husband and an ex-rock star turned rabbi. Unorthodox is the right word for this beguiling book.

The setting in Israel is so dynamic you feel as though you are there. To me, Brenda Barrie is the Amy Tan of the Jewish world, current and historical.

Barrie ensures we root for Marnie, whose intelligence level is genius, although that is no help in certain difficult life choices until she meets Eli, an almost equally complex man who shows her patience and love. With Eli she learns it's never too late to start a new life.

– **Janet Simcic**, author of *The Man at the Caffè Farnese* and *An American Chick's Guide to Italy*.

"Brenda Barrie's book *An Unorthodox Romance*, reminded me of Carol Shields' novel *The Republic of Love*. It is a story of second chances at life and love in a setting – in this case Israel, in Carol's book Winnipeg, Manitoba – that may not at first appear to lend itself to romance. This is a satisfying book, in which secrets are given up in order to make room for abundant life."

– **Anne (Shields) Giardini**, author of *The Sad Truth About Happiness: A Novel*

An Unorthodox Romance is a beautifully told story about facing one's fears and having the courage to let go of the past. Marnie had written herself off of ever being able to love again after a disastrous first marriage. But through the process of cutting the final ties to that relationship, she is not only able to love again but allows herself to feel worthy of being adored. Set in Israel in the late 1990s, Barrie's novel interweaves an ultra-orthodox community with a Reform rabbinical conference through strong and engaging characters. Marnie's difficulties in forgiving herself for the choices she's made will resonate with anyone who has struggled to let go of something in their past that holds them back."

– **Sidura Ludwig**, writing teacher and author of the novel *Holding My Breath*

Also By **Brenda Barrie**

THE BINDING (a novel 2005 & 2011)

THE RABBI'S HUSBAND (a novel, 2012)

Full Speed. Full Stop (poetry) 2003

This book is dedicated to
the late *Carol Shields*
my model in so many ways . . .
friend, mentor, author,
and winner of the Pulitzer Prize for
The Stone Diaries

A PERSONAL APPRECIATION OF CAROL SHIELDS

It was before I was a writer. Before I knew I was a writer, even though so many people have pointed out that my first job at eighteen was as a copywriter, and then as a journalist, feature writer, etc.

But that was not being a writer. That was just something I was able to do. It's a good thing I could do that one thing, because I wasn't a good enough typist for office work and numbers flummoxed me completely.

One day in the early 1980's I met Carol Shields, a 'real' writer. I was the chair of a national Canadian Arts Committee for Women and she was a member of the committee. She was deferring to me. I sensed something not quite right in the deference of this polite, quiet woman. Someone else on the committee told me Carol was a real author. Novels and poetry. She was deferring to me? There was definitely something wrong with that picture.

I went to the library and looked her up. (No Internet then.) She had written several novels. I read them all. Loved them: settings, language, tone, everything about them.

A few weeks later, there was Carol again, in the same book club I belonged to. We managed to make some members really angry. The club had originally been a very political feminist group. (We all remember the hotheaded 70's, right?)

Everyone hated the book we were reading. It was historical, and maybe a little literary, *The Greenlanders* by Jane Smiley. Everyone hated it except for Carol and me. The other members – as politically knowledgeable and active a group as you'll ever meet – were disgusted, claiming the two of us were turning the group into a literary club. Not a compliment in their minds, believe me. (Personally, I was never so flattered in my life.) And later when we drove home, Carol and I giggled about it. Also, it turned out we were near neighbors

If you met Carol in her later roles as a major literary prize winner, Chancellor of the University of Winnipeg, Pulitzer Prize winner, knowledgeable author being interviewed on the CBC, respected professor, you wouldn't think you could giggle with her. But you could.

Carol was amazing. She was all those things I've just mentioned, plus a loving wife, the mother of five, (one, a novelist, Anne, has written a blurb for me on this book, for which I thank her) and so much more.

One thing led to another. We became friends. Carol got some of my first poems published in a Canadian literary magazine, *Prairie Fire*. She asked me for information in my professional capacity that she needed for her Pulitzer-Prize-winning novel *The Stone Diaries*. She agreed to be my outside reader for my first manuscript, the thesis for my M.A, which later became my first novel, *The Binding*. In that capacity, as a member of the committee for my orals, she greatly confused my university in St Paul, MN, by being the 'real' Carol Shields.

Then we lost Carol to breast cancer. She had by then completed *Larry's Party,* later a musical too, and *Unless*, which, when completed, she told me, "I'm so happy I could go out and offer to take in other people's laundry."

She would have done a good job too.

Thank you, Carol, for playing such a major part in my life, so gracefully, seemingly so effortlessly. And thanks to the Shields family for allowing me to honor Carol in this way.

ACKNOWLEDGEMENTS

I'd like to acknowledge all the writers who are 'going it alone' now, finding ways to get into print, to find teachers, to find classes or critique groups, to find or create editors of their own, to get the book published, to get cover blurbs and well-designed covers. Then too, they have to get themselves noticed, to garner reviews or word of mouth, and of course, to find readers. And to do all this without agents, editors or major publishers.

It's a whole new world out there. The world of Amazon and Kindle, reading devices, books on tape and so many new forms of technology that in the months it takes to get this book into print (and available digitally) I run the risk of not mentioning something new and earthshaking.

I've done most of it. I've been lucky enough to have excellent teachers and, in a fairly timely fashion, to find small publishers. I've even had East Coast and New York agents who wanted to go to bat for subsequent books when the first one didn't sell. (Even Dan Brown's first books didn't sell.)

So for teachers: Lou Nelson and Daniel Levin, David Haynes (now a colleague) for critique groups in Orange County and Baltimore. For my most recent critique group. Janet Simcic, Dennis Phinney, Ana Arellano, M.J. Buist, John Gray, Ed Kaufman. Thanks to the Act IV conference, which so many of my critique group take the time to attend every year, plus David Speiselman and Corinne O'Flynn.

For this book, as always, friends and family who were advance readers: Virginia Sheff, Thea Iberall, Deborah Gall, Muriel Ashe, Joan Kaye and my daughter Renata Bursten, and double thanks to Rena Konheim who also created the covers for all three of my published novels. For authors who have offered me support and cover copy: Sidura Ludwig, Ann (Shields) Giardini, Janet Simcic and again, David Haynes. Thank you all for taking time from your busy schedules to read and to comment. And for the language consultants who helped me with French and Hebrew throughout the book, Rabbis Jon Konheim and Carla Freedman, and Andrea Pearlstein.

Thank you for dealing with messy manuscripts and finding the errors that would be embarrassing. Any errors that remain are mine alone.

And thanks to my family, Aviva and Joseph Cohen, daughter and son-in-law, and our nine grandchildren, a new grandson by marriage and, amazingly, a great-granddaughter.

Thank you to Gray Matter Imprints, for modifying their business several years ago from publishing only business books and adding novels, travel and essays. You gave several new authors such a wonderful platform.

And, as always, for my husband, Sid Bursten, who makes the whole enterprise possible, with his love and his always-boundless optimism.

Note on foreign language words:

Like my other novels, *An Unorthodox Romance* has no glossary. I have instead defined each foreign-language word immediately before or after its first use, just as I did when I was writing feature stories for daily newspapers, which made no allowance for glossaries.

Since the creation of the world,
God has been arranging marriages.

Yiddish Folk Saying

CHAPTER ONE

9:30 p.m.
October, 1997

Los Angeles, California

The single most important factor in what Marnie thought of as her escape from her ex-husband was the green light at the Mulholland on-ramp of the 405, heading south. She was even in the correct lane. Marnie, usually so careful, didn't give a thought to the implications of her action. She wheeled on to the freeway, joining the flow of traffic, telling herself: *Get to Tovah and Dan's house. You'll be safe there.*

She'd maneuvered to be first out of the *Yeshiva's* parking lot when the school closed, especially once she'd seen Shalom sitting in a red Voyager, obviously waiting for his host. Since many of the *Yeshiva's* teachers drove vans, she didn't know whose car it was. Probably, one of the teachers she distrusted the most. She knew there were a couple of teachers who misused their authority, their status, in the community. They charged the non-observant Jews they dealt with unconscionable amounts for their 'assistance' on matters like conversions, marriages and adoptions.

Had Shalom seen her as she'd escaped? He wouldn't expect her to be driving a car like this. Her dark green MG was one of her few indulgences.

Traffic was relatively light on the 405 South, a sign to her. She would be at her friends' house in a little over 90 minutes. Rabbi Tovah Feldner and her husband, Dan Goldin, had lived in California's far south Orange County for several years before Marnie moved back to the West Coast after one botched attempt in the late 1980's as a pulpit rabbi, and then several years of teaching Torah and Talmud on the East Coast.

Despite concentrating on getting away from Shalom at this moment, Marnie had already realized there was one way she could really escape. She could leave the country. If Shalom was in L.A., she could go to Israel, a trip she'd never made while he was in Jerusalem where he normally lived. There was even a decent reason to go. She'd just have to fool her best friend into thinking it was a spontaneous decision on her part. Certainly she couldn't suddenly tell Tovah the truth.

Marnie tried to settle into the flow of seventy-five mile-plus-per-hour traffic in the left lane, closest to the car pool lane. She could call Tovah right from the car. Even if she couldn't tell her friend the real story, she could probably convince her to let her come on their reunion trip. One of the rabbis had just cancelled because her children had chicken pox. Tovah could arrange to transfer that ticket.

Before dialing, she checked the traffic around her carefully, glancing into her rear-view mirror. A red Voyager van was right behind her. They were following her! Without a second's thought, her foot pressed down on the gas pedal.

Marnie tried to calm herself. Other than out-running them, her first option, she could change lanes and slow down. She could get off the Freeway at the next off-ramp, but she'd have to move all the way over to the far right lane quickly. In vain she looked around for a freeway sign. Where was she? Sunset? Wilshire? Venice? LAX? She was still in LA. Maybe they weren't actually following her. They could be going anywhere! Where were they?

She swiveled around, looking for the car, expecting to see Shalom's husky shape any minute. The red Voyager flashed by, entering the car pool lane right beside her. A Latino man and woman were watching her. Obviously she was driving erratically. She was running from her own ghosts, her own imagination. And there were a million red vans in L.A.

She could not stay in L.A. while Shalom was in the area. He'd made such a ridiculous demand. She couldn't figure out why he had said what he'd said. What could he really want?

She drove on, constantly checking, swiveling left to right, her eyes darting, looking ahead and then into the rear-view mirror. She had to do something drastic to escape. One sighting had been a false alarm. But the next one, or the one after that, and she'd be in real danger.

She punched the radio off. She'd hardly been aware of it until this moment. Elton John's "Candle in the Wind," was not going to help her right now.

Shalom had promised – no, he'd threatened – to come by her apartment on *Shabbat*, the Sabbath. She lived alone. She couldn't allow that.

His last blow had been years before, but Marnie's right cheek stung, remembering his open-handed slaps.

She could not return to the *Yeshiva* for her next class on Sunday morning. Shalom would accompany his host, one of her colleagues at the *Yeshiva*, to the student-led morning service. All the teachers attended. If she sat in her usual spot in the women's section, she'd be painfully visible. Very few women came to the service. If she missed it, she'd be just as obvious. Damn. Shalom already had her Los Angeles address. She couldn't hide at her parents' home in Santa Barbara either. It was the first place Shalom would go if she disappeared.

There was only one thing to do, and she had to convince Tovah to let her do it.

Still glancing left, right, ahead and behind, and despite the turmoil within, she punched the button on her car phone system, speed-dialing Tovah. She had to fool Tovah into thinking her chance to get away had just come up. She shuddered, thinking of Shalom, as she listened to Tovah's phone ring.

"You're calling to gloat," Tovah said. Tovah thought the usual opening chitchat of a phone call was a waste of time, even saying 'Hello,' if you already knew who was at the other end of the line.

"What? Gloat? What do you mean?" Marnie asked.

Marnie could imagine her friend, short and scrappy looking, her black curls all askew, talking on the phone while she did at least two other things.

"Because I've got to get all three kids ready so Dan can look after them for ten days, get all the laundry done, plus its Shabbat tomorrow night. So, I have to work tomorrow, and be at *shul* Friday night and Saturday morning. That means I'll have to pack before *Shabbat,* or really leave it until the last minute, after *Shabbat.* I hate to do that."

Marnie tried to make a sympathetic noise, but Tovah barreled on.

"And, while I've managed to get thirty-five rabbis to go to Israel for a 10th anniversary class reunion, I've failed with my closest friend. All the others understand we need to support Israel with tourism down, but you…."

"I'm glad to hear I'm still your closest…," Marnie said.

"That designation is only physical at the moment. You live the closest. I'm not committing to anything else right now," Tovah snapped back.

For the last two years, ever since the idea of their class reunion being held in Israel had been floated, and for the last year as Tovah had chaired the event, Marnie had insisted she wouldn't go, she couldn't go. Now, changing her mind at the last minute, she ought to expect to answer a million questions.

Then, Marnie suddenly knew what to say next. Still panicky, still hunting for a car following her, she managed to keep her voice light, almost humorous. Hiding years of your life from your friends made you an accomplished actor, or liar.

"Tovah, you know I support Israel as much as you do. And I feel bad about not supporting the reunion. So, we're both in luck. I find I can get away for at least the first week of the trip, maybe even longer. There's still a whole day before you – before we – would leave. I'll come right now. I'm in the car anyway. I can help you get ready, do the laundry while you're at work, organize things for you. I'll have all day tomorrow. We can have *Shabbat* and then leave. The plane is at midnight, right?"

There was silence at the other end of the line.

Finally Marnie had to say, "Tovah?"

"Our plane leaves at twelve forty a.m., a red-eye to New York. We'll meet in the morning for the El Al flight to Israel," Tovah said, automatically supplying the correct information.

She added, "You're in the car, coming here? You just packed up and left?"

"Actually I didn't even pack, but Belinda will do it for me tomorrow, and send the stuff along. I felt awful about refusing, and then you told me Cheryl had to cancel on top of that. I thought I should do something useful. You can transfer her ticket to me. You or Dan must have a t-shirt and toothbrush I can borrow for tonight. It was a whim of the moment, you might say."

"You can probably borrow Ari's stuff. He'll be taller than me by the time I get back," Tovah said absently, talking about her twelve-year-old son.

Then, quiet and very calm – in what the Feldner clan referred to as 'Rabbi mode' and without commenting on Marnie's supposed whims, which they both knew were non-existent – Tovah said, "Obviously, you've got a lot to tell me. Okay, Cheryl's bed and seat is yours. I'll need a check for the full amount. At least money isn't a problem for you. You'll be my roommate. There are no singles and I might be the only one talking to you after your continuing refusal. You, our *Talmud* star, and you wouldn't come. We'll talk more when you get here. I'll get the guest room ready."

"Right. Thanks," was all Marnie could manage. Tovah could see past the obvious. She was willing to take on trust that Marnie had to go to Israel. Of course she'd want answers, but she'd wanted answers for years. Now, relieved she still had Tovah on her side, Marnie dialed her housekeeper, leaving a long, detailed message asking her to pack for the upcoming trip, get a messenger service to deliver the suitcases to Tovah's, and take some paid vacation time.

She'd have to figure out something she could say to Tovah when she reached the sanctuary of her friend's Dana Point home. The list of things she wouldn't talk about was more important that anything she could say. She certainly would never tell Tovah anything about Shalom. Having had him in her life was bad enough. Running from him now, like – like – like any other frightened ex-wife, was too embarrassing. Tovah would probe, but in the end she wouldn't pry beyond the carefully posted "No Admittance" placards Marnie had in regard to her past.

The limits on her own story included not only her past with Shalom, but also what had happened with him earlier this evening. It also included why she could now return to Israel, something she'd never thought she'd do.

CHAPTER TWO

One Hour Earlier

Just an hour before Marnie was on the road to Tovah's, she'd been in her *Yeshiva* class room, as the usual two-hour Thursday evening *shiur* she taught ended. As she did after every class period, she sat, watching her teenage *Yeshiva* students file past the glass window of her cubicle. They were advanced students, the only boys she considered teaching, likely the only boys she'd ever be able to claim as 'hers.' Since the class was now over, they couldn't see her.

Marnie knew she would never marry again, so there would be no children of her own.

She stayed right where she was until every boy left the room. She could have gone when they did, but somehow it seemed wrong. Also, she liked to listen as they gathered in the doorway of the classroom to discuss the portion of *Talmud* she'd just taught in their three-time-a-week class. Did they think she couldn't hear them, because they couldn't see her anymore?

"But she said I was right!" Nathan was still defending a point he'd made in class.

"Only in those limited circumstance though. Your argument doesn't hold up in general. *Rav* Gershon says you can't...."

"You'll have to quote her if you think *Rav* Gershon is wrong."

That was Oscar, her best student, the one who always seemed to sense when she'd be looking up. When the class marched past her cubicle he often gave her a thumbs-up so enthusiastic she had to stifle her laughter. Would years of *Yeshiva* and postgraduate *Kollel* stifle his approval of her and her teaching?

Once Oscar even winked at her, and that time she had laughed, realizing at the same moment the whole class could hear. The walls of the cubicle they'd built for her, housing her and the electronic equipment they thought she needed to teach, only reached to a little over six feet and had no ceiling. Had they hired her without knowing she was five foot ten?

As the boys finally left she heard Oscar's voice ring out, fresh and young, "Have a wonderful evening, Miz Holland." Such daring was rare in a *Yeshiva*.

Most of the boys didn't speak to her if they saw her in the halls. In class they avoided her name as much as possible, just waving their hand until she spotted them through the cubicle's special glass window. Depending on which switch she flipped on her control panel, the glass could be mirrored, one-way or clear. If a student absolutely had to address her directly, he called her Miss Holland, in imitation of the other teachers at the school.

So far when they quoted her they just said, "She," or "Her." One day that would have to change. When you made a point in Talmud debate, you always had to quote your teacher. Long-term credit was what Marnie was after: "The scholar, Marnie Holland, says…"

Credits like that might actually change this traditional world where women sometimes taught, but were barely acknowledged. She figured it was less important they would never call her 'Rabbi.' Women were not ordained in the orthodox world. Maybe one day even that would happen.

The class members had finally gone, as far as she knew. She had to go by what she could hear, unless the students were right in front of her. Whoever had hastily designed her cubicle, once she'd agree to teach, had neglected to put in a window on the side opposite the door. She could only see the portion of the room where the boys sat.

If the boys were around, she couldn't even stand up and stretch, because she was so tall her hands showed above the wall, as though disembodied.

She knew each boy leaving the room would set his black hat, the crown low, the brim wide and flat, squarely on his head. All Turov males, not just the schoolboys, wore the same style of clothing, unchanged from the eighteenth century when the first Turov schools had been established in Western Poland.

Before she began teaching at this *Yeshiva* high school, she'd assumed *Turovers* wore their hats all the time instead of a *yarmulke*. But that was not the custom. Every classroom desk, in fact every chair in the building, had a shelf built in underneath, so all the men and boys could store their hats. Male *Turovers*, old and young, wore large black *yarmulkes,* silk or black velvet skullcaps, under their hats at all times.

In some ways this *Yeshiva* resembled an exclusive school like the British Eton. Like Eton, Turov had all sorts of archaic customs no one ever questioned. But, while Eton had done one or two things over the centuries to update their swallow-tailed and stiff white-collared uniforms, Turov had done nothing to change their clothing.

Did the boys ever consider that the garments they wore were modeled on the dress of Eastern European nobleman of the eighteenth century: knee-length black jackets, black gabardine pantaloons, long black socks, white collarless shirts, and black boot-like shoes?

If they were ever asked to picture Moses climbing Mt. Sinai, they'd probably visualize him in an outfit just like theirs, every single one of the five round black buttons on the jacket fastened, with the narrow band standing in for a shirt collar also buttoned right up to his throat. Never mind Moses' desert surroundings or his Egyptian roots. He'd wear his distinctive black hat squarely on his head.

Turovers did not acknowledge the climate in Southern California differed in any way from the weather in the old much-contested border area between Poland and Germany where their sect had first developed. They knew Moses would have ignored the climate too.

As far as Marnie was concerned, the clothing these ultra-observant men wore, just like the reasons they gave for why she needed to teach sequestered in a tiny little cell, were a prime example of confusing what was holy with what was merely archaic.

Turovers cited Torah and Talmud for their rules about women. Revered sources said that women did not sing in public. As a logical extension of that, women didn't speak in public either; therefore, they didn't teach. Probably for fear they would burst out in song. But, if a woman had special learning, one could have the knowledge present in the room, even if the woman had to remain hidden.

Marnie had special knowledge, a gift for understanding *Talmud*, the traditional mark of intellect in the observant Jewish community. Her part-time job at Turov, two evenings a week and a Sunday morning class, all taught from her special cubicle, was the result. When the Jewish community in Los Angeles learned she was in line for the most prestigious chair in Talmud at the University of Judaism, every other academic group also wanted her to teach. She'd shocked everyone by choosing this ultra-right-wing orthodox school as the one addition to her schedule, even though she was like a ghost in this room, either totally invisible, or only seen through the glass window of her cubicle.

She was a tall, slim young woman, younger than most people knew, with blonde hair and gray eyes, today wearing a tailored, pale blue suit. She could not have appeared less intimidating, exactly what she was trying to project. Marnie reasoned, if you are trying to accomplish something radical you should not telegraph your intent. Rather, you should look as non-threatening as possible.

Therefore, she made a special point of dressing well at the *Yeshiva*, always changing from the more casual clothing she wore to her real job. At the *Yeshiva* she wore properly modest suits and stockings. She did not cover her hair, but then no one in L.A. knew she had ever been married. In the traditional world, some divorced women got permission to uncover their hair, although many behaved as the married women they'd once been. Generally widows, too, kept their hair covered. Usually the women's rabbis decided.

If she'd felt comfortable wearing casual clothes at the *Yeshiva*, like a denim skirt or pants, with a t-shirt or blouse and a jacket, like she wore when she taught at the University, she'd have done it. If she'd known of some way she could have demolished her alcove, and all the rules, she'd have done that too. But, she'd decided she wanted to teach these boys. As their teacher, she would have an impact more long-lasting, much more subtle, than simply being visible.

When she was ready to leave, she cleared the cubicle window, not worrying about who saw her and who didn't. Her own image faded, and she suddenly saw him, sitting in a front row desk, as though he belonged there.

"They'll be quoting you as their *Rav* one day," he said. Her ex-husband! She hadn't seen him, hadn't heard from him in twelve years. He seemed to find something very amusing. The shock of seeing him was like one of the slaps he used to administer. Marnie spun around so fast she banged against the far side wall of her cell. She had to get out. It couldn't be Shalom.

She came hurtling around the opening at the back of the cubicle.

It was him!

'Twice as big as life,' she remembered her grandmother saying about someone's surprise appearance. He seemed to be at least twice as big as she remembered. When she'd first met him he'd been a sturdily built young man, barrel-chested, but fairly slim. Now a substantial belly rounded the barrel chest. He was still an inch shorter than she was, but now he had to be much more than twice her weight.

"Shalom!" She hadn't yet realized that she must hide her shock.

"Malka." How could he still insist on the name he'd given her?

"Not Malka. My name is Marnie." Despite her panic, her correct name seemed very important.

"Marnie is a *goyish* name," her ex-husband waved his hand dismissively, as he always had. "Also, it's a name for a child."

"It is my name, Shalom. Marnie."

"Marnie Holland, not Malka Gasith." How could he even imagine she'd use his last name?

"Well, if we were being totally authentic it would be Guberman, right?" she said. He never liked acknowledging his original last name.

Was he really so at ease that he didn't even stand up? Although he lounged back in his seat it occurred to her he looked somewhat uncomfortable. Also, he had a fading bruise on his left cheek and a scrape on his right hand.

Shalom didn't take part in any sports, and she couldn't imagine him in a fight. "Taking a new name in Israel, a Hebrew last name, is a fine tradition, even if the godless Zionists do it too," he said.

"Anyway, my last name is Holland," she said.

It sounded as though they'd calmly picked up the strands of an old discussion, but Marnie was anything but calm. Usually her fine, pale complexion didn't give her away, but right now she must have flushed a horrible shade of pink.

She stayed still, because anything she did might show weakness. Weakness in front of Shalom was out of the question, an invitation for him to strike.

It hadn't been necessary for Shalom to select a new first name when he came to Israel from South Africa. His parents had given him the English name of Samson, but his Hebrew name had always been Shalom, which translated to the favored greeting in Hebrew, 'hello', 'goodbye' and especially 'peace'. He'd told Marnie he would have picked the name anyway because Shalom, peace, was such an important value in Judaism. It might have been expressed constantly as people greeted each other; but there had been no peace living with Shalom.

Shalom had shown some imagination when he'd selected a new surname. Gasith meant granite, like the rock that must have been the substance of the Philistine's temple the original Samson had to destroy. Marnie knew him as rock: unyielding, difficult to move, impossible to destroy.

"So, Marnie, you haven't said it's good to see me. Or even that it's a surprise." Totally out of character, Shalom was attempting a light touch.

"It's a surprise," she agreed, her voice flat. She didn't move a muscle. Anything she did might be wrong.

"Well, it's good to see you." Why was he so conciliatory? Then he stood up.

Marnie took one step back on the dais, all she'd allow herself. "What do you want?" she said. "No, you can't want anything. There isn't anything you didn't take the first time."

Which way to go? Try to get out of the classroom? Go back into the cubicle?

"That's not true. There is something I want. I want a divorce. Apparently I need a divorce." He was at least ten feet away, but the expression on his face was unreadable, although he seemed to be attempting a smile.

How could he joke about such a thing? He stood there, hands behind his back, as though actually giving her a moment to absorb what he'd just said.

She looked at him carefully. Had something changed? His clothes were the same: a plain black suit, a white shirt worn open at the neck. His dense black beard had grown longer. It added some length to his face, which had become much broader; the effect of the years and of the weight he'd gained. His *tzitzit,* his ritual fringes, were visible, as were the black suspenders he'd always worn, and a belt. Naturally, he wore his own sect's black hat, with its high un-creased crown and narrow brim, almost the shape of a Homburg.

Then Shalom actually took a step backward. She'd never known him to retreat. Could he actually be uncomfortable? Likely he was just plotting. How could he turn the screw again? She'd met him almost fifteen years before. She hadn't seen him in a dozen years. She'd told herself all that was in the past. But, she'd left such a big part of her life behind her, in the hands of this man. He'd changed her life forever. She'd never risk marriage again under the kind of terms he represented. She realized it meant she'd never have a family. Being free of him had to be enough. To be free, and to have her work as a rabbi and a teacher, would have to be enough.

"You should see the children, our children," he said. Of course he'd found something wounding to say.

"Not ours. I wish they were mine; but they are your children. Two wives before me, two children. Thankfully, we never had any. If Sammy and Liora had really been mine, or, if I'd been able to stay with them longer, keep them with me, I might have been able to…." How might she have saved the children?

"Do what? You thought you'd reached them. But, if you saw them now you would know you never had any influence on them. Sammy – I mean *Shmuel*, is nineteen, and *Liora* is just sixteen. All their talk now is about their weddings."

"They're too young for weddings. And you've married too many times."

"Ah, Marnie, you're so hard, so cruel. If you were still Malka you would be kinder, more understanding."

"Shalom, I will not stand here and negotiate something when I don't know what is on the block."

He didn't seem to understand the word "block" as she'd used it. "A block? *Mah zeh?* What is that?" His English would forever carry the harsh metallic Afrikaans inflection that had always grated on every nerve in her body. But then he shifted to Hebrew. Originally, it was his beautiful Hebrew that had attracted her. He'd been an exceptional scholar of Modern and Biblical Hebrew, with a flawless accent.

His Hebrew had started their relationship.

But there wasn't time to think about that now. He repeated, "*Mah zeh?* What is this block?"

She forced herself to reply in crisp English. The first time he'd uttered a syllable in Hebrew to her, she'd been lost. She'd been looking for a teacher. It had been the first euphoric day of her first trip to Israel. She'd been standing on a corner in Jerusalem, map in hand, when a man asked if he could help.

She should have been immediately suspicious. But his appearance put her at ease: the black suit, black hat, and *tzitzit*, the whole costume reassured her. He was obviously *frum*, as rigorously observant as the rabbis she'd met at the American women's seminary that had sent her to Israel to study. They couldn't get over her rapid progress. That had been going on all her life, of course, since she'd learned French and Italian on a trip to Europe with her parents at the age of four.

But she was such a beginner as a real Jew. She'd still believed all *frum* people were moral, with perfect integrity. So it had to be safe to talk to him.

"You don't look like you're entirely familiar with the neighborhood," he'd said in Hebrew.

She would not think about their meeting. She dragged the conversation back to the stand-off of the moment.

"What's on the block is whatever you want from me, or from my parents. You can't have it."

"I want a divorce," he said again. How could he say such a thing, joke about something settled so painfully more than a dozen years before?

How could a man this cruel live? How could he walk abroad in the world without someone, even God, striking him dead?

"That's it," she said. "I thought everything you did to me in the years we were together couldn't be made any worse."

"We weren't just together. We were married, in case you've forgotten."

"We were. I have not forgotten. But you finally freed me, even though it cost dearly. It cost me years. It cost me the children. It cost them; God only knows what its cost them to be left with you. It cost my parents thousands and thousands of dollars. Do you think it's funny to come and suggest that you need a divorce? You, of all people? You always said that a *get,* a religious divorce, is all a real Jew needs. I suppose I should be grateful you didn't leave me a chained woman, an *aggunah,* the way some men do. But that wouldn't have suited your purpose. You wanted the money more than you wanted control over me. That's what you got."

Shalom actually looked abashed. He didn't try to say anything in his defense, which was unusual. Usually he was as prickly as any *sabra,* those born in Israel. The *sabra,* a cactus fruit, was reputed to have a honey-soft interior, even though it had thorns on the outside. Shalom was all thorns.

"Your custom-made religious divorce," Marnie said. "A *get* arranged for you by the same rabbi who came to Santa Barbara from Israel to marry us. Israeli authorities should never allow such things, but they do. I have my *get,* my kosher Jewish divorce. They sent me the papers, as required. All those certificates – my *get,* and our original marriage contract – all perfectly kosher and legal, if a little heartless, are in my possession.

"I'm lucky we didn't have the *ketubah,* the marriage certificate, beautifully framed the way couples do nowadays. Some of them are real works of art. Imagine taking it out of a frame, taking it off the wall.

"Anyway, we've had the *get* for years. We both wanted it, but I had to pay for it. What a system. I'm certainly not going to marry again that way, and I can't marry a non-Jew. There are no choices left to me. For you, a marriage seems to be a way to clear up your loans, any bills that you've accumulated."

She'd backed away from him, away from the outstretched hand he now held out to her, palm open. The gesture made it seem as if he really did need something from her. They were not married any longer, so according to the Law he couldn't touch her. He certainly did not need a divorce. Joking about it, taunting her, was just a way for him to be cruel, hurtful, without touching her. When they'd been married he'd been able to hit her.

In the matter of marriage and divorce, the State of Israel followed laws that had been protective of women thousands of years earlier, but gave few rights today. The Gasith divorce, the *get*, had been ready to deliver to her a few weeks after Shalom had finally agreed to grant it. She didn't even have to be present to accept the handwritten parchment. The state appointed a proxy. Once the document had been accepted for her, the two of them were divorced in Israel, and in the Jewish world. It was the only divorce that mattered.

CHAPTER THREE

Marnie had to appear strong if she had any hope of handling Shalom.

She straightened up. She stayed up on the dais of her classroom. He'd always hated that she was taller. She reached in to her alcove so she could pick up the school phone. With her fingers poised about the keypad she said, "You shouldn't be here. Just like in Israel, schools in this country have become very concerned with security. You can't just walk in."

He stepped up on the dais, came around to the back of her alcove. For a horrible moment she felt she'd let him trap her. But, he didn't come too close. He just put out his hand again. She couldn't help it; she flinched, as though he would strike her, as he'd felt free to do when they were married.

Much to her surprise, he didn't appear to notice she flinched. At least he didn't respond. Apparently he'd only wanted to stop her from using the intercom.

"Wait," he said. "Don't. We need to talk."

"I don't need to talk about anything," she said and then repeated. "You shouldn't be here."

"Alright, alright," he said. He turned to leave. It shouldn't be this easy. At the doorway he stopped, turned back to look at her. He gave her one of those smiles of his, thin-lipped, the way a snake would smile.

"I'm staying with a friend who also works here. It's near your apartment. I'll walk over *Shabbes* afternoon, and we'll talk then." There was another one of those smiles, but he actually left.

She heard his footsteps retreat down the hall. It had never been so easy. He would be back.

For the first time, her special cubicle felt sheltering. At least she was close to the intercom and could summon help. Even though the first floor of the school was empty, the building's lower floors weren't yet deserted. That would take about an hour, when the last class of the evening ended. Some of the boys were boarders from around the country, but they wouldn't hear anything, since they lived on the fifth floor of the building.

At the moment, standing in her classroom alcove, with the phone still in her hand, she could hear her own pounding heart, the matching pulse beating in her thumb, because she gripped the phone receiver so tightly.

She put the phone down but kept her hand hovering near it, just in case Shalom suddenly came back.

She sat down. For once she would have pulled the walls of her enclosed little space around her, to disappear inside its shelter. At the same time, she wanted to bolt for the parking lot and get to her apartment.

No, she couldn't do that. She would wait until the evening classes were totally over, the study hall closed. If and when she got up enough courage to leave, she couldn't go home. He knew where she lived. Even if he'd only pretended to know, the risk was too great. How could she believe he'd really wait until *Shabbes?* Shalom's word was worth nothing.

She'd finally left their marriage because, right after he'd promised the children would stay with them no matter what disagreements they might have, he'd punished her for continuing her studies in Hebrew and Talmud by sending them away, far to the south of Israel, to his aunt and uncle who lived in the desert city of Beersheva. He'd only let her speak to Sammy and Liora one more time, just long enough to make sure they were all crying. Then he'd cut off all contact.

All those people who think you're a genius should see you now. A real genius could think her way through this easily. A real genius would never have found herself in this position.

If she'd been smart enough, she'd never have let Shalom Gasith into her life.

CHAPTER FOUR

onday morning, with Marnie already in Israel, her parents, Walter and Beatrice Holland, were having breakfast on the patio of their home in Santa Barbara. They were waiting for a phone call from Shalom.

Walter Holland, tall and slim, fair-haired, with blue eyes, was still elegant in his late sixties.

This morning he wasn't even pretending he and his wife Beatrice were doing what they did every morning, going through the arts sections of *The LA Times* and, more important, *The New York Times*, before they opened their art gallery for the day.

Carefully balancing the cup of coffee his wife had just handed him, before he put it down on the patio table, Walter crossed his legs, unconsciously making sure the flawless crease in his silk trousers remained perfect.

Walter thought of himself as a latter-day Fred Astaire. If he could have carried it off in California, he'd have dressed the way Astaire did in all those elegant movies of the thirties, striped trousers and a grey cut-away. Maybe even spats. His friends would have laughed, so he opted for silk trousers, fine silk knit polo shirts or, his choice today, a perfectly tailored, British-made sports shirt in blue chambray, the cuffs and collar band lined with a coordinating paisley print. He also wore a cordovan leather belt and loafers made of perfectly aged leather, both hand-tooled in such a discreet pattern, so subtle, only Walter knew it was there.

His wife often commented that Walter was the best dressed member of the family, although with the expert use of cosmetics, a perfect wardrobe and the occasional attention of a friendly surgeon, Beatrice didn't look close to her age, mid-sixties. But on a day like this, worried about Marnie, her real age showed.

Walter wasn't aware of his clothing this morning, not nearly as much as usual. He was thinking about Shalom, his rotten, no-good, more-or-less ex-son-in-law, who would soon call and then come to the house seeking a favor.

He intended to enjoy every moment of the coming confrontation.

Beatrice and Walter had been shocked that Marnie was going to Israel.

"No, you can't go. It's too dangerous," Bea had said in quick response to Marnie's news. Bea, vivacious and striking looking, with grey eyes and deep auburn hair, always reacted to things quickly, often pointing out she didn't want to be bothered with facts.

"It's not dangerous there, Mother, the security is top-notch. The war has been over for years."

"Never mind security," Bea said. "I'm worried about Shalom, not politics." Her voice became tremulous. She sounded every one of her sixty-odd years.

"Please don't go anywhere near him, Marnie. Not even to the same country. Anyway, what about your teaching?" Bea dropped her voice even further, "Marnie, what did you tell Tovah and Dan?"

"You don't have to whisper, Mother," Marnie said. "Tovah and Dan are at work and the kids are at school. I'm alone here. The whole point right now is that Shalom isn't in Israel. As for work, I took some time. They expect this sort of thing occasionally."

Her parents knew that wasn't quite true, but they also knew Marnie had enough of a reputation so she could get away with a 'white lie.' She'd simply tell the department heads at both her jobs she'd mentioned this trip before. Since she was always believed, both schools would think they'd made the mistake.

"Did you tell Tovah...?" Bea began, but Marnie cut her off. "No, Mother. Neither Tovah nor Dan knows anything about my ever having been in Israel before I met Tovah there for the required first year of rabbinical school. They know nothing about Shalom. I gave Dan the keys and registration for the MG and told him to drive it until I get back. That stopped his questions. Tovah's used to not getting answers from me. She says I should have been a nun, complete with a vow of silence, not a rabbi. I promise I'll call you from Israel and keep you up-to-date on things. But, let me speak to Dad now."

Quickly Marnie told her father what had happened. "I don't understand what he means, claiming he needs a divorce. He's not crazy. If I poke around in Israel, I'll probably figure out what the hell Shalom really wants. In the meantime, he's likely to call you if he can't find me."

Walter knew what Marnie said was correct. Give his genius daughter a little more information or enough time to think things through, and she would certainly figure what had really happened when she and Shalom married in Santa Barbara. But, Walter wasn't going to worry about that now. He'd managed to outwit her on the question of her disastrous marriage, building in protections she knew nothing about. Right now he'd just enjoy the fruits of the plan he'd put in place. Marnie would appreciate it too, once she either figured it out, or when he decided to tell her.

✡

After waiting a dozen years for revenge, Walter found this last day, waiting for Shalom to appear, a real strain. He could still recall exactly how Marnie had looked when she came home, having left that *shmuck* after almost three years of marriage. No one hurt his brilliant daughter and got away unscathed.

When she'd first met the bastard, she'd called home. "Daddy, I'm getting married," she'd said over the phone, her voice high and excited. It was her first major trip on her own. She'd been just nineteen.

"Oh, no you're not," had been his instinctive response. "Not until we meet him. Not in a strange country. Don't do a thing until I get there."

When Walter left for Israel, within twelve hours of Marnie's first phone call, he had no plan except to delay things. Nothing Marnie said had reassured him. The guy, Shalom she called him, was poor. He'd been married before. There were stepchildren who needed her, a ready-made family. Walter didn't care if Shalom was a brilliant Hebrew scholar; that Marnie wanted to live an orthodox life, but most orthodox men wouldn't marry her because she hadn't been born into an observant family. All Walter knew was this: Shalom had to be bad news.

He might not have had a plan when he left L.A., but by the time his El Al flight landed at Ben Gurion airport, some twenty hours later, less than two days after Marnie called home with her news, Walter was well-armed.

People always said Walter Holland could start a conversation with a stone, could get a life story from a post.

Walter knew he was a lucky man, which was another way of saying he was an optimist. He'd boarded the airplane figuring something would occur to him, something would happen.

So, it might have been his conversational skills or that the man sitting beside him had never flown first class before and was overawed by the experience.

Rabbi Doctor Isaac Schlumberger thought everyone else had a far better right to be in first class. He was just a scholar lucky enough to be a guest speaker at a conference in Israel on the subject of women. 'Feminism,' he'd said, sounding as though a rare flu was loose in the world. "It affects everything these days."

"So, you'll be discussing marriage too," Walter had guessed.

That had opened a flood-gate. For the next twenty hours, almost without time for a nap for either man, and all during their layover in London, where Walter had insisted they visit the finest kosher restaurant for a meal – his treat of course – Rabbi Doctor Schlumberger delivered a discourse on American marriage law, Israeli religious marriage law (there was no secular marriage in Israel, Walter learned) and the differences between the two.

By the time Dr. Schlumberger got down to explaining the biblical origins of Israeli marriage law, originally planned to protect women and revolutionary in its time, Walter had a plan.

It had all started fifteen years ago. It was twelve years since Marnie had come home after leaving Shalom. So now, on his own patio, in the brilliant autumn California sun, Walter wished, perhaps for the thousandth time, that Marnie had stayed in science. She was brilliant, really brilliant. He couldn't help it, but to him Marnie becoming a rabbi still seemed the waste of a fine mind. If Marnie had come home from her disastrous marriage wanting to be a doctor, he'd have understood. After all, they gave a Nobel Prize for medicine, too.

The real truth was, when Marnie had finally come home from Israel, she'd been utterly defeated, spending several months going nowhere, doing nothing. Once her profound depression had passed, if she'd wanted to be an artist, a writer, anything, he'd have encouraged her.

At least the rabbinate had got her going again. The bad part had been she had to go right back to Israel for the mandatory first year the Reform seminary required. The Hollands had visited their daughter in Israel three times that year, concerned Shalom would hear she was in Israel or Marnie would panic and leave school, because she was worried he'd see her. Walter never told Marnie he was far more concerned she'd decide to get married again. She didn't know she couldn't marry again, at least in the U.S.A.

Walter had no intention of mentioning marriage to Marnie ever, unless she found a really nice guy. Then he'd tell her everything.

✡

Enough reminiscing, Walter thought. And then, the minute he didn't think he could handle waiting any longer, the phone rang.

"This is Shalom," he barked, demanding, "Where is my wife?" He didn't bother saying hello.

"Your wife?" was all Walter said. This guy was *chutzpah* personified. How dare he refer to Marnie as 'wife?'

"I'll find out where she is, you know." So far neither man had greeted each other or said anything else even vaguely pleasant.

"I'm coming to see you," Shalom continued. "I'll rent a car and be there in a couple of hours."

"My door is always open," Walter said. Both men hung up at the same instant.

Across the table from him, Beatrice raised one perfectly arched eyebrow.

"Payback time, darling," she said. Bea had an unusually well-honed sense of revenge. She would savor everything he told her, just as she had applauded all the planning he'd put in place to protect their daughter and to bring the whole situation to this moment.

✡

When Shalom arrived at the Holland's front door, Walter was alone.

Bea had not liked the idea of Walter meeting Shalom without anyone else present. "What if he..." she'd protested as Walter her urged her to leave for the gallery.

"He's not going to attack me," Walter said, sending her on her way. "First of all, he isn't the type. Second, once he knows the lay of the land, he'll realize I'm the only one in touch with Marnie who'll talk to him. I'm not going to tell him anything this time."

"We should have told her," Bea moaned. "We should have told her she's actually still married to him, at least in this country."

"If we'd told her, she'd have done the ethical thing, given him an American divorce, too. Neither one of them knew they needed it. They still don't know. You and I were the only two who knew then, and know now. We've kept it like this for good reasons. Believe me, if she'd needed to know, I'd have told her. There hasn't been one guy she's been serious about since she came home from Israel. I'd have told her she needed a divorce if she'd met anyone.

"Right from the first, ever since she had to go back for the first year of Reform seminary nothing has happened with men. She's terrified to marry again."

Bea had to agree. "There hasn't been anyone in her life since Israel. She wouldn't marry another Israeli. She was scared. Tovah told me Marnie never left the dorm the whole year they were in Israel. No one lived in the dorm that long, except Marnie."

"You've got to face it. If she'd wanted to go to Bangladesh we would have sent her. We couldn't have her moping around another whole year. If she wanted to be a rabbi, she was going to be one. You know your daughter. No one can change her mind about anything. She'll never get married again."

CHAPTER FIVE

Shalom Gasith used the same tactics in person as on the phone. He was barely inside the door of the Holland home before he said, "I want to talk to Marnie, right now."

"Well, she's certainly not here," Walter said, making a gesture that suggested Shalom check every inch of the sprawling three-thousand-square-foot, ocean-side home.

"I didn't expect her to be here," Shalom said. "I expect you to tell me where she is."

Instead of answering, Walter led the way to his private office off the foyer. This was not a social call. He was not going to offer this SOB anything to eat or drink. He knew from experience that except for highly distilled spirits in a crystal glass, his ex-son-in-law had always been quick to tell Walter nothing provided in this house was sufficiently kosher. Even if the food had been ordered from a kosher caterer, and served on paper plates.

In just the few steps it took to get to Walter's office, Shalom seemed to have re-thought his tactics.

"I really need to speak to her," he said, as though trying to explain something complex to a very simple man. "You'll never believe what she did to me, the trap she laid."

"Marnie laid a trap?" Walter said. He thought for a moment. "And all she caught was you? I guess it didn't work very well."

Obviously nothing was going as Shalom had planned. He stared at Walter as though he couldn't imagine how he'd come to be in this situation.

"She set things up. She arranged things. Somehow she's made it so that I can't get married again. My fiancée is waiting," Shalom said.

Walter sat down in his desk chair, gesturing to Shalom to take a seat.

"But you were married again. She told me. You let her know for some reason. You were gloating, I suppose. She worried about the kids. How are the kids, by the way? They were such nice children. Didn't your third wife like them? No, that had to be your fourth wife. Marnie was number three. Then you blessed another Israeli girl, didn't you? So she would be number four. Or did I miss one or two?"

Shalom looked daggers. "What business is it of yours?" he said.

"You're right. It's none of my business at all." Walter stood up again. "So, you came to see Marnie, but she's not here. She did call and tell her mother she'd let us know where she was, but I don't think Bea has heard from her in the last day or two. She's not nineteen anymore, Shalom. I don't know where she is every minute."

Walter walked over to the door of the den, opening it wide. "So, we've agreed. Whoever you marry is no business of mine. It was nice of you to stop by while you're in the country. When Marnie calls, I'll tell her you visited."

"Okay, okay," Shalom said. He sat down again in a low leather arm chair, Walter's favorite.

Walter sat down again in the executive chair behind his desk. It was much higher than Shalom's, more commanding. Walter didn't mind some advantage in this kind of situation.

"Marnie certainly had very little to say about anything after you married her. How in heaven's name did she manage to stop you from marrying again?"

Had he tipped his hand? Walter was anxious to know how much Shalom understood of the situation he was in. One thing he'd never underestimated was this man's intelligence.

Shalom went back to basic belligerence as a tactic. "I want to know where Marnie is. Right now! My wife," he repeated.

"You divorced her," Walter pointed out in his softest voice.

"Apparently she didn't divorce me," Shalom said. Now his round face was red, his eyes had narrowed.

Walter made certain he looked confused by what Shalom was telling him. "She didn't have any right to instigate a divorce. You explained it to me. She told me the same thing. The Israeli authorities agreed. Divorce was only possible if you initiated it. All I got to do was write the check. A twenty-thousand-dollar check if I recall correctly, the going rate for a religious divorce, a *get*, at that time. *Get*, a funny word, considering. Of course I don't know much Hebrew. I only know Marnie had to get a *get*. She still has the damn document in a safe deposit box somewhere. In case she ever wants to remarry or something. So she can prove she has a *get*. Get it?"

Walter appeared very thoughtful for a few minutes, as though considering nothing more than the vagaries of the two languages. Then he said, "I'd have offered you double if you'd let her see the children on some basis. I'd have gone to fifty, even a hundred thousand, if you'd let her have custody. They were such nice children."

He sighed heavily, as though the children probably weren't so nice now. Walter looked up quickly enough to see a greedy look flash across Shalom's face.

"But you kept saying you didn't want to benefit from the irreconcilable breakdown between the two of you. You only wanted your expenses. Plus something for your loss of wifely love and support. Hard to believe a girl, barely twenty-one – she really was just a girl then – could be so valuable. Especially since you'd sent the children to your aunt and uncle in Beersheva, and Marnie couldn't even see them. She said she only left after the last conversation you allowed, all three of them crying."

"Malka should have…" Shalom began

"Don't you dare call her Malka. It's not her name. The last thing you ever did was treat her like a queen."

Walter had meant to keep his cool, but he'd lost it when he heard Shalom use the Hebrew name he'd given Marnie: Malka. It was a symbol of everything he detested about this man. He'd taken a beautiful name and idea, a queen, and put it to such base use.

Before Walter realized it he was standing, his fists bunched at his side. He had to fight to regain his control. Think like Astaire, he told himself. Quickly he sat down, letting his chair spin back and forth a little, a substitute for wanting to take a punch. He'd noted Shalom had a pale bruise on his cheek, and the remnant of a black eye. He hoped it had really hurt when those blows landed.

"It's not her name," he concluded.

"So, you're not going to help me," Shalom said.

"Did I say I wouldn't help? I don't remember saying that," Walter said.

For a moment Shalom looked hopeful.

"But, since you ask, no, I'm not going to help. And, if I don't hear from Marnie very soon, I may tell the cops you're in town and you threatened her. Why are you suddenly asking me where she is? You were the one who saw her last, at the *Yeshiva* where she teaches."

"She told me about your visit the last time she called. Now I don't know where she is. You claim you don't know where she is either, but you're the one who saw her last. Maybe you're just trying to cover up what you've done to her."

He stood up, walked over to Shalom sitting in the low leather chair. "Where is my daughter?" he demanded.

Shalom looked at Walter as though his ex-father-in-law had lost his mind.

"How would I know?" Shalom said. He stood up, almost stumbling, as though to get away from a lunatic.

Walter went to the door of the den again; opened it and walked out into the foyer. He crossed the honed marble floor, pulling open the heavy front door of the house. "For the moment, I'm going to believe she's okay. I'll give her a day or two. Not more. You'd better hope she's okay.

"But, if you don't know where she is, and I don't know either," he continued, "Why are we having this conversation?"

As Shalom left, Walter let the door slam.

Walter knew a parent never quite finished raising a child. When the child is unique, a Marnie, it was more work than most.

CHAPTER SIX

Summer, 1963

When Marnie was four, Bea Holland decided that she and Walter would turn their annual European trip, usually a whirlwind two-week buying trip for their Santa Barbara gallery, into a family vacation. For Marnie's sake they would extend their trip to a month, one week each in France, Germany and Italy, and a week to travel. They would let their agent in England take care of acquisitions there. They would bring along McKenna, Marnie's nanny, who'd been with them since Marnie was born.

Nanny McKenna, originally from Great Britain, would leave them at the end of the trip, take her own vacation to see her family in England and Scotland, and then fly back to Santa Barbara.

The night before they were leaving Santa Barbara, McKenna brought Marnie to say good night to her parents and their guests. Bea and Walter were having a little farewell dinner with friends before they left for New York in the morning.

Nanny said, "In the nursery we're that excited about our big trip beginning tomorrow."

After kisses and hugs Nanny and Marnie left the room. The Holland's friend, Celia Aronovitch, said, "I keep wondering how on earth you ever found a nanny who sounds like an extra from the British theater. Most of them speak Spanish, not English."

"You have to have a child like Marnie," Walter said complacently. He leaned back in his chair, trying to look even more debonair than usual.

Debonair or not, Beatrice kicked her husband under the table.

He yelped, "Ouch, why did you do that?" while rubbing his ankle.

"I don't want you to brag about Marnie when there is even the remotest possibility she can hear you," Beatrice said severely.

"Then you'll never be able to say a word," said Celia Aronovitch. "She must have the ears of a hawk, and be able to see around corners and up and down stairways. The things that child knows. She's got to be eavesdropping."

"Celia, you're mixing your metaphors horribly. It's the eyes of a hawk," her husband Ed protested.

"Eavesdropping? Not Marnie. She just knows. What did she tell you?" Walter said.

"The other day she gave me a very complete tour of Europe, via the globe over there."

"She wasn't playing with it, I hope," Beatrice said. "I've told her not to. I made the mistake once of showing her where we live on it. It's early 19ᵗʰ century, for God's sake. She'll cover it with fingerprints."

Celia Aronovitch sighed. "To raise a child like Marnie is a challenge. I thought mine were brilliant at five because they could turn on the TV and find Romper Room on their own."

"She's not five yet. It's just the child of older parents…" Walter would have finished his sentence but those at the table did it for him.

"Is always more intelligent," they chorused.

"Walter," Ed Aronovitch said. "This is not a case of more intelligent. I mean even Celia, who is Marnie's godmother, forgets how old she really is. She could easily be six, seven, even older. You two waited forever to have a child, and then you happened to luck out. She looks like Shirley Temple and she's got a mind like… like a college professor."

"She told me the name of about ten of the countries," Celia reported. "When I complimented her on remembering France, England, Italy, Ireland, and so on, she said she could read the rest of the names to me, if I wanted her to. She said, 'Aunt Celia, when you can read, you don't have to remember.'

"By the way, Bea, I thought you said you weren't going to let her learn to read so early. You said it's too hard to socialize a child who already has all those skills."

Beatrice Holland changed the subject. "We've all know that kids memorize story books and so on. So, why not the name of different countries, if that's what interests them? I mean, she knows that we're going on a big boat, far away, across a different ocean." Beatrice waved at the dining room window and at the Pacific Ocean only about a hundred yards away, and by extension, at the Atlantic too.

"But Bea, she also said that one of the countries had the same name she did. I made a joke of that. I said I didn't know there was a country called Marnie."

"She said, 'Auntie Celia, you shouldn't make me laugh. This is important. The country is named Holland, not Marnie. It's right here.' She put her finger right on the Low Countries. I don't think that globe actually says Holland. So, I suppose she couldn't have been reading it."

The Hollands looked at each other across the table. Marnie could read. They didn't know whether to be pleased or worried. They had specifically told McKenna not to teach her. She would be entirely too far ahead for even their area's excellent public schools. McKenna claimed she had not taught her charge, but she'd also said she didn't know a way in the world to stop a child so determined to learn.

Walter had taken their daughter aside a few days later and asked when Nanny had taught her. Marnie had looked troubled and said. "Oh, Daddy, I don't think Nanny can read at all. I think she just knows all the storybooks by heart. When I ask her to teach me, she always says she can't. So I learned it myself."

Within minutes of embarking on the *Ile de France*, Marnie made a very troubling discovery.

The ship had just pulled away from the dock. First-class passengers had been invited to a reception in the somewhat over-decorated gold and white Grande Salon.

Marnie prowled around the large, beautifully appointed room for a few minutes. To McKenna, Marnie appeared troubled. The nanny wondered if her charge might be seasick.

At McKenna's urging, Marnie did agree to make a selection of items from the lavish buffet table. Marnie sat quietly, eating and obviously listening to something, or for something. When McKenna asked her a question Marnie urgently put her fingers to her lips and shook her head. She said, "I'm sorry, but I can't talk to you now."

That was worrisome to the nanny. Marnie tended to be a chatterbox. Her nanny kept trying to engage her attention, totally unsuccessfully, when Beatrice Holland arrived.

Marnie said, "Mommy, you have to tell Nanny to hush. I need to listen."

"Marnie Holland, you apologize to Nanny immediately."

Marnie was smart enough to know she couldn't cross her mother. She apologized.

When Marnie's apology had been accepted, her mother said, "What are you listening for? Any noise you hear is probably the wind, or the ship's engines."

"No, Mommy. It's the people. Lots of them aren't saying their words right at all. I can't understand them." She'd looked so troubled that her mother relented and said, "What do you mean, Marnie?"

By now Walter had joined them. Marnie took her parents' hands and, walking between them, with McKenna trailing behind; she led them over to a couple nearby who were speaking to each other in rapid French.

"See," she said. "She understands him. And he understands her. But, I don't." She had the most tragic expression on her face.

Her parents never thought of laughing.

"Darling, they're speaking a different language. They're speaking French," Bea tried to explain.

By now the pleasant middle-aged couple under scrutiny stopped talking to each other, to smile at Marnie. She'd always been accustomed to this sort of attention from adults. She'd returned their smile.

"I am Jean-Claude Margarit, and this is my wife, Annette," the somewhat roly-poly man said, in English. He extended his hand to Marnie, then to her parents.

Marnie tugged at her father's jacket. "Daddy, ask him why he speaks that way."

"You will have to excuse my daughter's curiosity," Walter said. "Your French surprised her. She doesn't understand you, of course."

Jean-Claude Margarit leaned over the small table in front of him, to speak directly to Marnie. "You see, it's very convenient to speak two different languages. I can say, 'you are a very pretty little girl,' or, I can say that you are '*une jolie petite fille.*'"

"And, I can say, 'thank you,' or I can say..." Marnie said promptly.

Behind them Annette Margarit, a small intense looking woman with dark hair and eyes, dressed in the most extreme high fashion sports clothes, murmured something, but no one paid any attention.

Jean-Claude said, "You can say 'thank you' or you can say '*Merci, beaucoup.*'"

"*Merci, beaucoup,*" Marnie repeated. "What if I wanted to say the table or the chair, or this big boat?" she asked, putting her hand on each object in turn, indicating the ship with an encircling gesture.

She had mimicked his *merci beaucoup* perfectly, and then asked her next question with such aplomb Jean-Claude was momentarily nonplussed. His wife leaned over and said. "You can say *la table*, or *la chaise*, *ma petite.*" She gestured to the two objects in turn, to make her lesson clear. "And this big ship *is ce grand navire.*" Annette had a very pronounced accent, Russian, not French. "And *'ma petite,'* means 'my little one.'"

"Merci beaucoup," Marnie smiled at her. The two sets of adults looked at each other with shared consternation. Jean-Claude said, "What a good memory you have, *ma petite.*"

He didn't get a thank you that time, in English or French, just a tiny smile.

"Daddy, how come no one taught me *la table* or *la chaise*, only table and chair?" Marnie crossed her arms over her chest, as though now angry.

McKenna stepped in. "Your father cannot be teaching you fifty ways to say the same thing. There are too many languages, and people don't learn them all at once."

"But I need to know," Marnie wailed. "I need to know." She began to cry as though a great tragedy had befallen her.

"Zie bleiped a kindt." In colloquial Yiddish, Annette had observed Marnie still behaved like a child. Beatrice Holland was trying to comfort and silence her daughter. She had gone down on one knee. She looked up at Annette and said, also in Yiddish, "Of course she still behaves like a child. She's only four. I don't know what to do with her."

Marnie stopped crying for a moment and glared at her mother. "You just said it different too! You can't do that! I don't know that way to talk." She stamped her foot at each word: stamp...stamp...stamp...

Around them people had quieted and were turning to stare. McKenna didn't care if Marnie had just asked to have The Theory of Relativity explained to her, in French or in any other language. Her concern was behavior.

She'd gathered her best starchy Scottish-English nanny manner around her and said, "Miss Holland; that will do. You are to beg pardon this instant. Then, we will go to our cabin. Later, when we are calm, and more ourselves, we will discuss French lessons with your parents."

It was an inspired thought. Marnie gulped, sniffled once or twice, took the pocket hankie McKenna offered her.

Without another tear falling, she said, "Someone will teach me more *la table, la chaise, ce grand navire?*"

The nanny looked at both the Hollands, focusing on Walter. "You can't stop it, sir, when they want to learn. I believe I have pointed this out before."

Walter Holland frowned, a lot more frightened than proud at that moment. "You go with Nanny now, sweetheart. Yes, if you want to learn *la table, la chaise,* we'll find someone to teach you. But, just a few minutes a day. This is supposed to be our vacation."

Marnie put her hand in McKenna's. She smiled at the Margarits, particularly Annette, sensing she had an ally there.

She said; her accent still perfect, *"Merci beaucoup,* Daddy." Then she stopped. What was wrong with her sentence?

Annette understood immediately, and provided the words. "You say, *'Merci beaucoup, Papa. Merci beaucoup, Maman.* To your nanny, you say *'Merci beaucoup,*

Nourrice McKenna.' And to us it is, *'Merci beaucoup, Monsieur Margarit, Madame Margarit.'* And then you say*, 'au revoir;* that is, good-bye for now."

Marnie repeated all of her new information once, to herself. Then she turned and repeated it again, out loud, each phrase addressed to the correct adult. She was waving happily, repeating *"au revoir,"* over and over again, as Nanny McKenna led her out of the Grande Salon.

After Marnie had left the room, Walter sat down heavily in an extra chair beside the Margarit's table. "Will you excuse me if I sit here for just one moment?"

"Yes, certainly, please sit. You will join us? We will chat." Jean-Claude got up and pulled out a chair for Beatrice, who sat down beside Annette.

"And your little linguist; what is her name please?"

"You must excuse Marnie," Beatrice started to apologize.

"Please do not," Annette Margarit said. "She has a formidable brain." Annette's sentence was polyglot. She spoke in English, but she'd pronounced formidable in the French manner and used the colloquial Yiddish word *'kop,'* – literally 'head,' – instead of 'brain.'

"You'd be the one to give her lessons," Beatrice said somewhat vacantly. Then she turned to her husband. "We'll not have one minute of peace. And she'll be speaking French before we're off this ship."

As if the two couples were friends of long standing Annette put her own hand over Beatrice's. "I will sit with her fifteen minutes, morning and afternoon, for a lesson. Why not? It will be most amusing. To teach that one, Marnie, it's a *mitzvah, non?*"

"But no Yiddish, please, good deed or not. I had enough Yiddish as a child." Beatrice said. She didn't even think to protest that Annette wouldn't want to spend time with a four year old.

"So, why not teach her Yiddish?" Jean-Claude laughed. "Although I myself do not speak it, it was my wife's childhood language."

"Mine too," Beatrice admitted. "That's why not."

Walter Holland said, "I don't understand a word of it either. So, there will be no Yiddish."

The four adults looked at each other and laughed, already friends.

Every day during the trip Marnie visited Annette for fifteen minutes before lunch and again before she ate at the early dinner seating with her nanny.

The adults sat together at the late seating. On their second night out Beatrice had hastened to apologize to Annette. "You must have thought me ill-bred, ungrateful. Not to thank you for being willing to be bothered by Marnie, for actually volunteering. I was…"

Jean-Claude said, "No. No. Her two visits, they are making the most amusing half hour of the day."

Annette reassured her, "You must not concern yourself. We were all a little shocked. And, she persists with this. Apparently she is asking everyone for words.

"Also, she wants to know why the *le* and *la* and *les*, and what these words means. When I tell her, then it is why is the table and the chair a girl, but the boat a boy? And do all things have their own *le-la*? I tried to explain gender, a little, and also, nouns. Yes, I said, you need to know the *le-la-les* for all things. And, we've agreed that the verbs – she calls them the running, sitting words, because those are the first two that came up – at any rate the running-sitting words are tricky, but they do not have a le, la, les.

"I'm terrified to teach her wrong—she'll grow up and sue me. Also, already she wants to know why my accent is different from Jean-Claude's accent."

"I told her it was because we came from different countries," Jean-Claude said. "I hope that I did not make an error in saying this."

"There's no point in trying to hide anything from Marnie," Beatrice said gloomily, as though speaking about some all-knowing adult.

Walter, equally glum, reported, "Nanny says she follows the help around as they work, asking what is this and what is this: the bed, the floor, the lamp, the soap, the dishes, the cup, the saucer."

Annette knew the results of Marnie's questions. "And she remembers. She remembers everything. I think you will have to apply for a tutor while you are in France. Perhaps, we can find someone who could travel with you."

"My God, I can't do business with an entourage," Walter moaned.

Annette turned to him. "Do not distress yourself, my friend. Our son will find one of his friends who is without employment for the summer. We will say only the most clever can apply. You cannot stop such a '*kop*.' She will have to be taught."

"McKenna's been saying this to us ever since Marnie learned to speak before her first birthday. I always hoped she was just trying to let us know what a fine nanny we had," Beatrice said.

"I thought so too," Walter admitted.

"It's not the worst problem in the world," Annette pointed out. "Although it no simple thing; to know what do with such a child."

By the time the Hollands had completed their trip, Marnie was speaking passable French, some German and a little Italian.

On the way home, again on the *Ile de France*, Beatrice had found Marnie staring fixedly at one of her books and murmuring to herself. She'd thought Marnie was just reading the book aloud, until she heard what her daughter was saying. "It's the cat in English and *le chat* in French. It's *le chat* in French and *die katze* in German. It's *die katze* in German and *il gatto* in Italian."

CHAPTER SEVEN

September, 1980

Marnie remembered the *Ile de France* trip and her introduction to French, Italian and German with the greatest affection. Her introduction to Hebrew was considerably more traumatic.

As the youngest PhD student in biochemistry at Stanford, a teaching assistant just past her seventeenth birthday, she had assumed her major professor sitting in on one of her seminars early in the semester was routine. Professor Blumenthal knew her, but she doubted he'd ever seen her handle a class of new students. She'd be supervising some of these students directly one day.

What surprised her was a summons to his office the next morning.

"We've had a complaint lodged against you," he said, seeming very troubled.

Blumenthal was almost a caricature of the absent-minded professor-scientist. He was clearly displaced from his native New York. His accent was much stronger than the trace accents she occasionally heard from her New York-born parents, plus the professor lacked any of her parents' sophistication. Blumenthal was rumpled, with too-long hair and a graying beard.

Marnie waited. She mentally reviewed yesterday's seminar hours. It wasn't the brightest group she'd ever met with, but nothing stood out in memory.

"George Anton says you pick on him."

"George Anton is not prepared. He shouldn't be in the program. I mentioned him to you when we met him the first time."

"Well, possibly. We'll know better in a month or two, I suppose. But he says you deliberately pick on him. He says you're anti-Semitic."

Blumenthal, Marnie thought. Her parents had mentioned the name was Jewish. Obviously he can't believe I'm anti-Semitic.

"That would be like saying you're anti-Semitic," she said, and smiled.

"Miss Holland, if true, this isn't particularly amusing."

"Well, considering, maybe it's not so amusing, but it is silly."

"Silly? Amusing? You find such a charge, even a hint of it silly or amusing? Racism, anti-Semitism, has no place…"

"Professor, I'm Jewish too. How could I be anti-Semitic? I'm anti-unprepared, I'm anti-dumb. I didn't even know he was Jewish. Is Anton a Jewish name?"

"You know Blumenthal is a Jewish name. And what is Jewish about your last name, Holland?"

"My parents said your name was Jewish when I mentioned it to them last year. As for Holland, I don't know. I just supposed my family came from there at one time. We're from Santa Barbara now. My parents are originally from New York, like you. I'm not, we're not...very Jewish. It doesn't come up very often. I didn't know he was Jewish. And, why would I care?"

But, apparently Stanford cared a great deal. There was an inquiry, a formal hearing and ultimately, a dismissal of the charges. At the end of the semester Mr. Anton left the University program, exactly as Marnie had suggested he should.

Marnie was left with a strongly worded 'request' from the University Regents that she had to fulfill. Although her parents protested the injustice along with Marnie, they'd all agreed it wasn't worth a fight or a court battle. And, as Marnie said later, it had been her opportunity to learn Hebrew. More than once, her parents wished the whole thing had never happened.

The university required Marnie undergo something new, 'sensitivity training.' They put her under the direct supervision of the Hillel rabbi. Rabbi Dan was a modern young rabbi. He seemed like an especially hip young professor. His office had books on three walls. On the fourth wall there were some drawings of old Jerusalem, guitars, bongo drums, and a certificate from The Union of American Hebrew Congregations in Cincinnati declaring him a rabbi.

For all his modernity, and the fact he later became a good friend, Marnie discovered he was extremely old-fashioned when it came to Jewish education. He was also old-fashioned in one other way. Rabbi Dan had a deep love of Yiddish, so Marnie had a chance to learn something of that language too.

Unlike every other academic she'd ever met, he was not especially impressed with Marnie's stellar academic record.

"It says here, 'a genius.'" He peered at the file the University had provided, then at her. She realized he was younger than she'd first thought.

"Geniuses, we have; many, many geniuses. A scientific genius. Very nice. Very important. But, not a Jewish genius, right? Jewishly, an ignoramus."

Marnie flushed. The word had never been applied to her before. Could there even be such a thing as a genius in Judaism, she wondered? Later she was grateful she hadn't asked.

Rabbi Dan found her woefully deficient in what he considered important; a standard Jewish education, any knowledge of the Bible beyond a few selections as literature. She had no information on the Hebrew Bible, the Five Books of Moses, and no knowledge of Hebrew, not even the ability to read a prayer book.

"Both your parents are Jews? How can it be? You've never been in a synagogue? You don't know which way the prayer book goes? In your schools, no one's Jewish? Not a friend? A cousin? Is Santa Barbara *yudenrein*, free of Jews?"

Marnie knew enough German and twentieth century history to be repelled by such a suggestion. "Of course it's not. But the private school I went to, and with all my extra tutoring, my friends – I don't have that many – are older. Then I went to college in Santa Barbara. I was young; so my parents wouldn't let me go anywhere else. I didn't know who was Jewish. Maybe if their name was something like yours, Cohen, or something. And, why would I ask? No one ever asked me," Marnie protested.

"I know you read Hebrew in the other direction, but it was instinctive to open the book the regular way when you handed it to me. I was at a Bar Mitzvah once in New Jersey, and a wedding. But, also a confirmation. No one there asked me if I was Episcopalian. So, why would they ask if I was Jewish? It doesn't make any sense."

"And it's true you look like the California girl personified," Rabbi Dan observed. "So, you're right. Why would anyone ask you? They'll ask if you play beach volleyball. That's what they'll ask.

"So, you'll be a good *maidel*, a good girl. A few more 'relationship' classes you likely don't need, but you'll go. So, in addition to Jews, if you run into different kinds of Christians, Baha'is, Muslims, Hindus, Buddhists...let's see what else, aha, Sikhs... and one meeting for everyone else, if anyone else is left. Then you'll come back to me, and we'll begin."

Marnie wanted to ask, "Begin what?" but she didn't.

Marnie discovered that she was not unique in 'beginning' as an adult. All over the country young adults who had been raised by free-thinking, liberal Jewish parents longing to escape what they thought of as the repressive Sunday school experiences of their own childhood had neglected to educate their children. Marnie had become a *B'aalat T'shuvah,* one who returns.

"It isn't reasonable to call me that," she protested. "I can't return to what I didn't know."

"Nevertheless, that's the term," the rabbi said, and he introduced her to other students like her, unlettered in Hebrew, totally lacking any knowledge of Torah or Talmud.

So when Rabbi Dan opened the Torah, the Five Books of Moses, at Genesis and read, from one translation, "In the beginning," then stopped and spent two hours on those first three words in English (one word in Hebrew, B'rasheet), and explained the problems that arose from the various translations, traditional and modern, and on later misunderstandings from studies in Latin and Greek of the same text, Marnie was well and truly hooked.

She had begun.

By the time she had mastered Hebrew, modern and Biblical, which, as usual, took her about six months, and had been introduced to Talmud, which required more study, Aramaic and Rashi Script – specialized Hebrew named for a 11th century C.E. scholar who'd lived in Troyes, France, most of his life – she was very far from the beginning and nowhere near the end of Jewish studies.

Marnie had waded into the great 'sea of the Talmud' and knew she would be swimming in it the rest of her life. The Talmud was almost two thousand years old; the history of her people was likely double that age. The modern history of Israel spanned much less than a century.

Compared to this new world she had discovered, even advanced bio-chemistry – as challenging as it might be – was a walk on the beach.

CHAPTER EIGHT

Jerusalem, Israel, October, 1997

Marnie almost gave herself away to Tovah one of the very first moments they arrived in Israel.

The two women had passed through the King David Hotel's stunning lobby, with white and gold capitals on the colorful Egyptian-style pillars. They had not even fully unpacked when Marnie said, "You'll be busy with conference details. I'm going to run around a little this afternoon and renew my acquaintance with the sights of Jerusalem."

"Renew?" Tovah said. "You never left the dorm when we were at school here. You only went somewhere if there was a class trip or if your parents dragged you out when they visited. No one else lived in the dorm all year. You always said you'd come back one day and do it properly, but you were going to focus on school for the year. It turned out you were the only one of us who didn't need to study like mad, yet you were constantly at it. What do you mean: renew?"

"Well, metaphorically," Marnie managed to say and then was deeply grateful when the phone rang and claimed Tovah's attention.

Damn, she thought as she waved in the most light-hearted way possible to her friend and room-mate, leaving before Tovah could question her further.

She didn't stay in the elegant area around the King David Hotel, which, despite its exotic décor, might have been a hotel in any cosmopolitan center.

Instead she took a cab, heading for one of the business sections of Jerusalem, just outside the walls of the Old City. Tovah, like anyone she'd met after she'd been married to Shalom, knew nothing about her earlier history. Tovah only knew Marnie had been a PhD candidate in bio-chemistry, had discovered Jewish texts, dropped her advanced degree work, and gone into the rabbinate. It all added up, if you assumed she was well into her twenties while working on her PhD. No one realized she'd only been eighteen and almost finished with graduate school. She'd barely been nineteen when she met Shalom and twenty-one when she ended her marriage. No one in her present life knew about those few years; the years that had completely changed her life.

She had been a very young rabbinical student, but no one knew her real age. Marnie never discussed her age, or her personal history. She had exorcised the three most difficult years of her life as much as possible. As a result she had never really dealt with them.

✡

At first, Marnie couldn't even find the building in the Nachlaot area of Jerusalem. Nachlaot, built in the late 1870s, one of the first areas outside the gates of Old Jerusalem, was rich with history. Synagogues lined its winding streets, restaurants and shops with signs in Hebrew and Yiddish as well as English, jostled each other for space. Here and there a larger building, built in the late Victorian era when every city in the world tried to look like London, stood several stories higher than the other buildings.

Her seminary had been one of those – a women's school when she first arrived in Israel. She wasn't sure why she wanted to see it again, but probably her meeting with Shalom made her want to evaluate what had happened. Finally, she figured out which building it was. It had been redone, but it was still a school, a new *Yeshiva*. A small brass plaque below the nameplate said, "Educating Men and Women."

"Not in the same classroom, I bet," she muttered under her breath.

The façade of the building had once been done in an excessively over-decorated style, the beautiful golden Jerusalem stone madly carved into dryads and nymphs. Now someone had made an equally ghastly choice and had given the building a metal façade like a giant automobile grille.

One thing was certain. Security was a big part of the building now. To get inside she had stare up at a camera, give her name and state her business, at the request of a disembodied male voice. "I went to classes here once. I just want to look around," she said, before she could push through a double set of weighty Lexan and metal security doors. All concerns for security seemed to stop there. No one was around.

Behind the updated façade it was the same building. She was in the same huge rotunda, four stories high. She'd stood beside Shalom that first day, looking up at ranks of stairs circling above. Now she seemed to be on an echoingly empty, deserted stage set. When she'd been here before the place teemed with students and teachers.

She was about to turn to leave when the figure of a tall man seemed to almost fold himself over a railing three stories above, waving, as though desperate to get her attention.

"Don't leave," he yelled, sounding almost frantic. The echo of his voice bounced around on the stone floor.

"Why not?" Marnie responded, looking up. She had to shade her eyes from the noon-day sun streaming in through the transparent roof. The roof was new, as though whoever had redone the building had plunked an old-fashioned conservatory on top of this Victorian-era cast-iron building. The new roof must have been done at the same time as the modern metal façade. She hoped the roof was bullet-proof and bomb-resistant Lexan too.

Everything was backlit at the moment, so all she could see were the many staircases reduced to spider web tracery, and the outline of one man. The man's face was invisible. What was clear from his antics was his determination she not leave.

He made some sort of gesture, either waving or suggesting she come upstairs, she couldn't see clearly.

Then he said something, possibly in answer to her rhetorical question. But, since he turned and ran down the stairs at the same time, a trick of the building's acoustics made it seem as though he arrived before his answer, which, it turned out, was not very convincing, just, "because…well, because."

Once he was on the first floor the two of them stood there looking at each other. For someone who'd been so determined for her to stay, he didn't seem to have much to say, just, "Because I have no one to talk to up there."

It didn't sound like a casual pick-up attempt. For one thing, he didn't look the type. For another, he actually sounded desperate.

"I'm not anyone to talk to. I was in this building once before. I'm out sightseeing and wanted to visit again. I'm guessing you have none of the old records."

"You can't go sightseeing from here. It's far too hot even for October. Most things close for the next two hours anyway."

"Well that's true but…

"So there must be something I can do for you." the man persisted. "Some service you require. How about a class? You took a class here before. You're looking for a refresher Hebrew class, right? When we have enough students we're going to offer great classes."

The memory of Shalom recognizing her as a student so many years before made her bristle. It wasn't this man's fault, but still. "I don't need a class," she said in Hebrew, very abrupt.

Her discomfort at being reminded of Shalom made her abrupt. This man looked at her so beseechingly she might have signed up for the class just to do the *mitzvah*, the good deed, of putting him at ease.

This is silly, Marnie told herself. Obviously just thinking about Shalom made her hypersensitive. No telling what trying to track down his children, her one-time stepchildren, would do if she let it get to her. She couldn't go on seeing an enemy around every corner, or being rude to perfectly inoffensive people. This man seemed more inoffensive than most, so awkward and gangly.

He couldn't have been more different from Shalom. He appeared to be about her age, in his thirties. He was tall, at least six four. He was not handsome. His features were oversized and his Adam's apple was hugely prominent. He had light red hair and the kind of very blue eyes that strong sunlight would turn sapphire. His hands and face was so freckled the effect was of a slight over-all tan.

His dress proclaimed him at least somewhat observant. He wore a hand-knit skullcap in light blue, and his trousers were light gray polished cotton. Instead of the usual white shirt he was wearing a short-sleeved, light blue polo shirt exactly matched to his skullcap. Some woman, probably his wife, cared enough to make him a *kippah* to match his clothing. He was carrying a very limp-looking navy blazer.

"I'm a rabbi," Marnie said. She could hear the sharpness in her voice. She was daring him to proclaim he didn't recognize women rabbis. "I'm here for a conference. That's why I don't need a class."

Her interrogator didn't seem to miss a beat. "You're a rabbi," he said. "That's good. I'm a rabbi, too. Maybe you'd like to teach a class here sometime?"

"A woman, teach here?"

"Why, don't you approve of men and women teaching and studying together?" he said. Suddenly the shoe was on her foot.

"Of course I approve of men and women studying together. I'm just surprised you do." How had he put her on the defensive?

She hurried on. "Anyway, you don't have classes. You said it's only an offer to teach if you had students." Then she was sorry to have attacked. He looked so depressed.

"Actually I said when we have students."

"Well, it wouldn't be possible anyway. I won't be here long enough to teach. I teach at home, in L.A. I only came in to look at the place again. I don't need…"

She was going to say she didn't need a thing, but he had other ideas.

"You need lunch. I need lunch too. At least I can offer you a meal, even if I can't offer you students. Students might be a problem. You always worry no one will come. Well, it doesn't matter. You can tell me what you teach while we eat something. I'm starving."

At a dairy restaurant two blocks away Marnie ordered two fruit blintzes with sour cream. Her companion ordered a four-course meal.

"This is my main meal of the day," he said as he started on thick mushroom and barley soup. "I don't have much of a kitchen. I can't really cook, anyway. Plus, it's nice to have a colleague for company."

He thought of her as a colleague. It made a nice change from the rabbis at the *Yeshiva* back home. It must be very depressing not to have any students. She settled in for an extended lunch hour.

Two hours later, having watched him devour an amazing amount of food, she had eaten her two blintzes and had indulged in two tall glasses of iced coffee, one with ice cream, one plain.

Rabbi Eli Altman had the trick of getting her to talk, something most people could not accomplish. But, having asked her what she taught and where, he began eating steadily and didn't say another word. She had to say something.

Finally she said, "Okay, I've explained. It's your turn."

"Oh," he said, "Nothing I've done recently is as interesting as what you do. I can't believe that in addition to the University of Judaism you teach at a Turov *Yeshiva*. I couldn't do it. But I must say you have good reasons. I like your thinking. They wouldn't hire me, but they hired you. You must be a *talmidat hachamim,* a female Talmud genius. It must drive them crazy. They won't come looking to make me an offer. I'm not that good."

Seemingly very comfortable with this pronouncement on his skills, he paid for lunch, refusing any contribution from her. They walked outside. He looked around as though there were great dangers at hand and he had to defend her.

The afternoon sun filled the street with short, thick, black shadows, but it was still too early for much foot traffic. At first glance it might have been a quiet corner in any major city. But the signs on the buildings were Hebrew, and every street sign was in Hebrew, Arabic, English and some French, a left over from a colonial period still honored.

There were many young soldiers around, part of the Israeli Defense Force (IDF), all of them wearing dusty green uniforms and heavy sandals. Most of them were off-duty, but Marnie knew Israel Defense Force rules required them to carry their weapons at all times, in case the country had to mobilize instantaneously.

Every solider, men and women, most of them eighteen to twenty years old, carried an Uzi rifle slung over the shoulder. So it wasn't really quite any quiet street corner. It could only be Israel.

"You shouldn't stand around here bareheaded in this sun." He seemed genuinely concerned, as though he planned to walk along beside her to provide the shade he felt she needed. Then he asked, in the tone of an anxious parent, "Do you even have sunglasses?"

Marnie pulled her glasses out of her bag while Eli began rooting around in a fanny pack he had slung around his waist as they'd left his *Yeshiva*.

First he handed her a small pad of paper and a pencil. "Here, I need your address and phone number so I can call you." She was so bemused by his combination of diffidence and bravado she wrote down her name and the name of her hotel, then handed the note pad back to him.

"You can't go walking around without this," he said. He pulled out a small tube of sun block and squeezed some out onto his fingers. For a second she thought he was actually going to apply it to her nose and cheeks, but just as his hands came close to her face he seemed to recall himself.

Suddenly all the bravado was gone and he was a confused man who had overreached. Without saying anything she offered him her hand instead of her cheek. He transferred the creamy white lotion onto her fingertips. The lotion smelled like Israel, oranges and almonds. Her companion blushed enough to obliterate his freckles.

He's shy, she thought. Most of this is some act he's developed to hide it.

Whether he was shy or not, he regained his composure quickly and said, "Good," as though he'd accomplished everything he'd had in mind.

He stood beside her watching as she applied the sun block he had provided, then he said, "I'll talk to you soon."

He turned very abruptly and set off down the street, his long-legged stride carrying him back toward his empty *Yeshiva*. He looked back over his shoulder once and smiled.

Even if his technique with women was awkward, he'd learned a great deal about her. All Marnie knew about her colleague, this tall, skinny, somewhat homely rabbi, was his name, Eli Altman, and that he had a job for her if his school ever had enough students.

CHAPTER NINE

arnie had only part of one day before the conference began, and she intended to make good use of it. The next morning, without letting Tovah know exactly what she was doing, she left their room early.

She would find her one-time stepchildren today. She'd have to become a spy, confirming that Shalom wasn't back in the country. She'd wanted to see how Sammy and Liora had turned out. She hoped by seeing them she'd know if they would welcome her into their lives, or if they would immediately call their father and tell him she was in Israel.

After considering various costumes to disguise herself she decided the way she looked was disguise enough. No one would consider a tourist who didn't cover her cropped blonde hair, even one sensitive enough to wear an ankle-length broomstick pleated skirt and a gauzy blouse with modest three-quarter length sleeves, could once have lived in Mea Shearim, amongst the *haredi*, the orthodox Jews of the district. She looked like what she was, a tourist dressing appropriately for this area so the locals, members of various orthodox Jewish sects, would not hate her on sight, be tempted to throw a rock or scream she was a 'daughter of Israel' and should dress modestly.

Shalom would not have moved from his home in Mea Shearim. His house was the settlement he'd received from his first wife, Sammy's mother. The house had been the price of the first *get* Shalom had bestowed; the house and custody of Sammy.

When she got to Mea Shearim it looked the same; like a small *'shtetl'*, or village, in the Pale of Settlement in Russia, the only place the Jews had been allowed to live in that country. In Mea Shearim the houses were gated, most built of stone, not wood, but the effect was still of a grungy European village from the time before World War II decimated the Jews of Europe.

She knew there was a small row of shops, a few stores and a café, at the end of Shalom's street, creating an excuse to hover in the area. She wasn't certain how long she could make her shopping expedition last.

Several of the stores were the same as when she'd lived there. The one new business was a shop, *Zahav*, the name advertising that they dealt in gold. Apparently they bought old gold, jewelry, gold teeth, cheap broken necklaces and so on, offering loans like a pawn shop, or outright purchases. Marnie remembered the shop had once been a book store. The sign in the window said the shop was closed until the end of October.

The first store in the row was the biggest, perhaps twelve feet wide. It sold kitschy Judaica to tourists, when there were tourists around. The Intifada had been over for years, but tourism was still affected.

The resulting cut-backs in staff meant one lone girl, about fourteen years old, was in charge of the whole shop. She was obviously very orthodox, wearing what Marnie and most of the world thought of as the *frum* girls' uniform: an almost-ankle-length denim skirt, a white blouse with three-quarter sleeves, knee socks and heavy-looking sneakers.

The girl was anxious to make a sale, but she went back to reading Psalms once Marnie convinced her that before she bought anything, she planned to stand there and read every amulet, every prayer, every description of the supposed demon Lilith, every talisman against the evil eye.

Marnie was actually able to keep 'shopping' for almost forty minutes, all the while standing close to the door of the store, so she could watch the street. When she really could not stand to read one more word of blurry Hebrew, she went next door ready to spend another hour or more pretending to dither over the choice of a *tallit*. She'd even go so far as to buy one, she decided, although another prayer shawl was the last thing she needed.

Ordinarily she'd never buy anything in the kind of shop where she had to invent some mythical man she was shopping for: husband, brother or father. In Mea Shearim no one actually admitted any woman ever wore a prayer garment.

She'd worked her way through the classical wool prayer shawls and was beginning on the silk models when a long arm reached over her shoulder and a familiar voice said, "Would you like me to model this one for you?" It was Rabbi Eli Altman. Running into people you'd just met was not so unusual in Israel, Marnie knew.

Israel was a very small country. Today Rabbi Altman was wearing light blue jeans, a white polo shirt and the same hand-made pale blue *kippah* he'd worn yesterday. Maybe the woman who'd made it for him had selected blue to match his eyes. He had the bluest eyes.

The young male clerk in this store–apparently the merchants were all using teenage staff as a money saver–was too young to have even the beginnings of the required beard. He was also obvious enough to look very relieved once Marnie had a man with her.

Marnie had been vague about what man she was shopping for. She'd only mumbled 'mmm' when asked if it was for husband, father, brother or perhaps–the clerk had grinned at her when he made the suggestion–maybe it was for some lucky man who would be her *chatan,* her bridegroom.

"Comes the *chatan,*" the young clerk said, seeming personally pleased, as though he was responsible for making a match, a *shiddach,* for Marnie.

"Just go along with the idea," Rabbi Altman muttered under his breath. "We're not going to change anything here. I've been watching you. You're killing time here. I am too, but I tried to start at the other end of the mall. The gold shop is still closed."

The idea that a strip of a few stores and a tiny café, most no more than ten feet wide, adding up to a 'mall,' struck Marnie as very funny. In order to spy on Shalom's children did she really need the protection of a man? She knew nothing about her companion. The last man who had picked her up in Israel had been Shalom. He had been the biggest catastrophe in her life. Had she learned nothing in the last fifteen years?

Somehow, all this serious thought, the idea of the little, narrow store fronted by a stone sidewalk and a cobblestone road – no green thing growing anywhere – making up a mall, Eli Altman and a teenage boy hovering over her, made Marnie do something totally out of character. She found herself giggling. She started to laugh. Then she found she couldn't stop. After a minute or two, eyes tearing, she let Eli Altman steer her outside which he managed to do without seeming to touch her. He found her a chair at a table in front of the tiny coffee shop next door. How odd to let her guard down around this man. Normally she didn't trust anyone that much. Before this she would have choked before she'd let herself laugh like that, or demonstrate any vulnerability.

Eli disappeared into the café, so small there hardly seemed room for customers. A wide glass- fronted refrigerator and a counter-display case full of pastry seemed to take up all the space.

Eli returned carrying a handful of paper napkins, two small bottles of water dewed with cold, and a tall beautiful glass filled with an iced coffee and ice cream concoction, the whole drizzled with dark chocolate.

"This is as good as any sundae," he promised Marnie as he set it down in front of her. The bitter fragrance of coffee and dark chocolate melding with the sweet vanilla scent of the ice cream made her mouth water. In her haste to avoid Tovah she hadn't eaten breakfast before she'd left the hotel.

The proprietor of the tiny shop followed Eli outside. He set down a similar iced coffee creation for Eli, this one slathered with caramel syrup, deposited two plates of luscious looking cake on the table, collected his money, and left, after adjusting the umbrella to protect them from the sun.

Having accomplished this, what was notable about Eli was what he didn't do. He didn't make small talk. He didn't ask her what she was doing here.

Now she couldn't think what had made her laugh so hard in the store. Fortunately, she didn't have to explain. She just tasted the chocolate hazelnut torte in front of her, and the drink.

"Delicious," she said, and Eli nodded in agreement. Marnie felt herself relax, a rare sensation for her, especially around someone she hardly knew. What kind of magic was there in this man?

Normally Marnie let whoever she was with carry the burden of conversation, but here neither of them had to think of what to say. They both seemed content, or at least relieved, to sit in silence. Finally, just as Marnie put her fork down on the glass plate–she was going to have to say something, sooner or later–up the street from where she and Eli were sitting, the gate to Shalom's house swung open.

Two young people walked out onto the street, Sammy and Liora. Would she have recognized them anywhere else?

Liora had been four when Marnie left Israel. Now she was sixteen, tiny, barely five feet tall. She was beautifully shaped, wearing the same uniform as most other girls her age: ankle-length skirt, blouse, knee socks, sneakers. Her curly medium-brown hair had been tamed into a fat single braid flipped over her right shoulder.

Her brother, Sammy – his real name, *Shmuel, had* hardly ever been used – had been almost eight years old when he and Marnie had wept a tearful goodbye in the last telephone conversation Shalom had allowed. Now he was a young man, a taller and slimmer version of Shalom when he was younger.

Sammy wore the black suit, white shirt and black hat of every other man in Mea Shearim. Somehow, Sammy's version looked 'hip.' The collar of his white shirt wasn't limp and flat the way most were. Rather it stood high, crisp and flared. His suit seemed trimly tailored, the black fabric rich, not shiny. The suit fit well, acknowledging Sammy's form beneath.

The young man wore his black hat with its high un-creased crown and narrow flat brim with the flair of a cowboy angling his Stetson, or a diplomat with a top hat.

The two were in a far more intense conversation than usual between a brother and a sister. They walked, ignoring everything else, their heads together. They were coming directly toward the café. There was so little car traffic on their street they walked right down the middle of the cobblestone road, narrower than a back alley in the U.S.A.

They'll move over to the stone sidewalk when they're in front of the café, Marnie thought. Then they'll be right in front of me. I could practically reach out and touch them.

The pair stopped in the middle of the road, perhaps twenty feet from Marnie and Eli Altman, so Sammy could light a cigarette. Without thinking, Marnie reached out her hand, as though the gesture would stop him from lighting up. How could Shalom let him smoke?

Liora didn't seem to share Marnie's concern. She used the pause as an opportunity to reach under the collar of her blouse and pull out a key she wore on a chain around her neck.

Marnie was trying not to stare. She didn't want Eli to note her interest in these two young people. What could she say to him to explain why she cared about two people who ought to be strangers to her?

To her surprise, Eli wasn't paying any attention to her. Instead of sitting as he had been, slumped in his chair, a posture that hid his unusual height, he was in the act of standing, slowly rising from his seat in a deliberate manner, like a flag ascending a flag pole. Clearly he meant to draw attention to himself, and it worked. The few people on the street, the cafe owner who was bringing coffee and cake out to other customers, a couple of young mothers with prams parked beside them, and especially the two young people, Sammy and Liora, all had their eyes riveted on him.

There was no question the young Gasiths had seen Eli before. Liora saw him first. She clutched at her brother's arm before she remembered herself. Men and women, even brothers and sisters, did not touch in the orthodox world. When Liora grabbed her brother's sleeve, she stopped the lit match inching toward the cigarette in his mouth. There was an instant when Sammy tried to shake off her hand, but then he saw Eli and froze. He also knew the tall red-head. Seconds later the burning match nipped at his fingers. Sammy dropped the match and stood, seemingly hypnotized.

By the time Sammy's match hit the ground and went out, Liora seemed to recover from her surprise. She slipped the chain from around her neck so she could use the key easily. She marched past Eli, stopping for one moment to stare into his face. To Marnie's surprise, she made the most distinct and very disrespectful Israeli sign against the evil eye right in his face; then continued walking, using her key to open the door of the locked gold shop. Marnie swiveled in surprise to see Sammy, rather than waiting for his sister, had run away, or at least had disappeared down the road and swung onto a bus waiting there. How could Shalom allow his children to take city buses? They were so dangerous, so often the target of terrorists. Where was Sammy going? What was Liora doing?

The girl was only in the shop a few minutes. She came out holding a small stack of envelopes and carrying a handwritten list. Again, like a small but brave puppy confronting a Great Dane, she walked through the crowd in front of the coffee shop, this time coming close to, but finally skirting Eli. Without looking back she marched up the street toward the same stop where her brother's bus still waited. She got on the bus, joining her brother at the back of the vehicle. The bus pulled out. Through the back window Liora made another gesture, also obscene, although more universal, as the bus pulled away from the stop.

"She's got more guts than her brother or her father, that's for sure," Eli said, more to himself then to Marnie. He sank down into his seat.

"I hope they end up at Hadassah Hospital," he continued. "And that they wanted to go in the other direction. They're probably going... Who knows where they're going? And, who really cares? Some other *schlemiel* will have to deal with them now."

One thing was clear. Marnie had no explaining to do. Eli Altman wouldn't know she had any interest in the pair of youngsters.

Eli seemed to have suffered a total loss of the energy that only a moment ago had compelled him to stand. He kept staring straight ahead, avoiding Marnie's eyes. She sat slightly off to his right. Finally he swiveled a little to meet her gaze. He'd blushed bright red. Even his ears were pink. His dark glasses shielded his eyes but he still had trouble meeting Marnie's gaze.

"You probably wonder what this is all about. Those two are the reason I'm here. Bumping into you was just good luck."

Being flirtatious was the last thing on Marnie's mind, but, even in her present state of confusion, it pleased her to hear he considered meeting her good luck. It had been a long time since a man had expressed any interest in her, or she'd allowed it.

"It's a long story," Eli said.

Marnie glanced at her wrist watch. "I've got all the time in the world," she said. Surprisingly it wasn't even noon.

"Let me just check one thing, while you decide what you want to do next," she said. She got up and walked up to the door of *Zahav. T*he sturdy safety glass door protected an office consisting of one room with two desks and a small counter for customers. Information in Hebrew and English said, 'Shalom Gasith and Son.' There were two other company names listed. This was Shalom's business headquarters.

When she returned Eli had slumped in his small chair.

"I only wanted to get married," he said. Marnie waited for more, not saying a word.

"Those two, they're not husband and wife. They are sister and brother."

Marnie nodded. He would assume she was simply taking in his information, not that she'd ever met these two young people before. Eli had shifted his chair so it faced her more directly. Marnie didn't want him to change his mind and not tell his story.

"You wanted to get married," she prompted in a very soft voice, as utterly devoid of emotion or judgment as she could manage. Obviously he was still single. Was that good news, or...? She told herself she wouldn't go there. Not yet. "It didn't work out," she prompted.

Eli nodded.

Finally he said, "It didn't work out. And, it didn't really start here. It just ended here."

CHAPTER TEN

Ⅰf you really don't want to tell me why you're here, or, if you don't want to talk about it at all, that's okay," Marnie finally said, when Eli had remained silent for several more very long minutes. She had to let him off the hook. As much as she'd like to know his story, he didn't owe her any explanation.

"I don't think I cannot tell," he said as though he suddenly understood a deep personal truth. "I've got to tell somebody. I've got to tell you."

Marnie's heart gave a little quiver when he emphasized the word 'you.' But, she couldn't stop to consider what the vibration deep within might mean. She could deal with the fact she felt relief. They could focus on his problem, whatever it might be. She'd kept so much of her life private. She wouldn't have to divulge anything, not tell him why she was there, or worse, tell him a lie. Too bad they couldn't just sit here in the sun and have no problems needing discussion. They could joke, even flirt a little. Could her life ever be so simple?

"I would never speak to anyone else about a private matter," she assured him. What did he want to tell her? "Anything you say will be safe with me."

"Let me show you something," Eli said decision in his voice. He reached for his wallet in one of those awkward male gestures, trying to fish it from his front pocket without standing up. His motion lifted the table between them a little. The tall iced-coffee glasses and the spoons shivered against each other, playing a little tune.

Finally he pulled out his wallet, and, after rifling through one of its side pockets, he extracted what seemed to be a small photo. He placed it on the table face down, first making certain the table was dry and clean.

"I have to tell you a whole lot first. For instance, you have to know I used to be the lead in the rock group, SerpentSity."

Whatever Marnie had been expecting to hear, this wasn't it. She continued to stare at him as though he'd eventually say something making sense. She looked around. What he'd just said couldn't be more at odds with the quiet street, with the men in strict black and white walking to the bus stop, with the women shopping, each one wearing some sort of head covering. Maybe Eli had said something completely different and she'd misunderstood him.

Finally she repeated, "Serpent City?"

"City with an 'S' and run together," Eli said, exaggerating the edges of the sibilance of all the "S's in the name of the group, as though pronunciation was what really mattered.

"Okay, City with an S, Sity, all in one, if that makes a difference. SerpentSity."

"I had to find the one girl who has never heard of me," Eli said, although her lack of knowledge actually seemed to please him.

"I think I have heard of the group, but I wasn't much for rock music."

"At least I'll always know you were never one of my groupies." He seemed cheered, relieved; as though Marnie not knowing about his first career indicated her good taste.

"Marnie, you have to have had some exposure to popular culture, even if you went to a Catholic girls' school and entered rabbinic school from a cloister."

"Not exactly," Marnie laughed. Her own story was odd, but not that odd.

"Actually I was fourteen when I went to college," she said. "I may have been young, but I wasn't dead. But that's another story."

Eli looked only mildly surprised. "Okay, I'll need to hear about that. But, you've barely heard of SerpentSity or their lead singer."

"They're the group that wore makeup all the time, snake makeup," she said, recalling some details of the group's publicity. It seemed so unlikely to be talking about snake makeup when the three women sitting at a table next to them were speaking to each other in rapid-fire Yiddish, with every hair on their head modestly covered. Despite the heat they wore heavy lisle stockings. They could have been from a Polish village of a hundred years ago, except she'd seen one of them checking a pager. Time and history were elastic in Israel. How would you say SerpentSity in Hebrew or Yiddish anyway, Marnie wondered idly?

"Right. Python, cobra, rattler, you name it. I was Rattler."

Visualizing outlandish make-up patterning Eli's homely, boney face actually wasn't difficult. Those angular planes – she'd heard people like Eli described as Lincolnesque – would have made such a disguise almost attractive.

"So, no one knew what you really looked like?" She needed to say something. She had never before been the one with the ability to fill awkward gaps in conversation.

"Why did you stop?" She tried again. If she asked enough questions, eventually it would be his turn to speak.

"Probably because of the thing you just said. I realized I had forgotten what I really looked like." He reached over and flipped up the picture on the table.

The moment Marnie saw it she remembered. Eli's picture was a miniature full-color reproduction of the cover of one of the major weekly newsmagazine. The masthead of the magazine had been cut off, but the legend beneath the picture was clear even in Eli's small reproduction. It said: *The Bad Boy of Rock Tells Half of It.*

The cover showed a much younger Eli, with the left side of his face and his neck the canvas for a pattern of dramatic brown and white rattlesnake diamonds. Even his red hair on the same side had been sprayed to match the rattler markings. The right side his face was naked. He was shirtless too, which added a powerful sense of vulnerability and exposure in the picture.

"So you were a successful rock star," Marnie said. "It's unusual, but it's not a crime." It occurred to her that given their surroundings, 'bizarre' might have been a better word than 'unusual.'

The man in front of her didn't seem to really hear her last comment. Now she could see his blue eyes were bright with embarrassment. He had more to say.

"This picture saved me. This picture, and all the deaths."

"You had a lot of deaths to deal with? Deaths and this picture saved you?" Questions really were the easiest.

"Well, the picture first. It was a known the whole group did their makeup from the top down or the bottom up, across the width of their face. So it would be even. And, we did it ourselves. That was one of our *shtick*. As you said, so no one really knew what we looked like."

"But in this picture, the makeup is only on one side," Marnie observed.

Eli nodded. "I'd agreed to do a cover. They'd asked me if I'd do half my makeup. It would be a sensation, they said. Later I realized they assumed it would be the top half or the bottom half." His left hand moved, bisecting his face horizontally, covering first the top half then the bottom half; demonstrating what the magazine had expected.

"For some reason, for some good reason, this one time, I did it this way." He reached up again, this time using one long-fingered hand to vertically cleave his face in two. "I really don't know why I did it."

"And your misunderstanding of what they wanted told you something?"

"It told me I was in danger of being ripped in half. The group disbanded two months later, with an album at number one."

"And then you went home and wanted to get married?" Marnie guessed.

"It wasn't nearly so simple and I didn't think about getting married then. I'd left my family years before. For a few years I'd actually managed a double life; daytime at a High School *Yeshiva*, nights in the clubs. I think the fact I hid it all hurt my parents as much as anything.

"Marnie, when I did this, in the years I founded and starred in SerpentSity, I was a loathsome person."

"Loathsome is a very strong word," Marnie said.

"But accurate," he said. "For almost a decade I certainly did loathsome things. I did drugs. I wrecked hotel rooms. I had groupies, lots of groupies. My family almost gave up on me. I was like a lot of people in the rock and roll world. You've read about it all: drugs, sex and rock 'n' roll? And people dying from it."

Marnie shook her head. She had heard, although she had no direct experience. "Some of your friends died?"

"Well, several people died. Never mind the famous ones, Joplin and so on. I didn't know most of them personally of course. But Lenny Breau, Freddie Mercury, Andy Gibb. I knew some of them. Plus people you've never heard of."

"They all overdosed?"

"No, but drugs and alcohol played a big part in their deaths. My family sent me a list. Right near the time this magazine cover came out."

"Your family did? That's what stopped you?"

"Well, something stopped me. I suppose I finally grew up, too. You know, my father and all my brothers are rabbis. Some of them are famous. I come from what is usually termed a rabbinic dynasty. I don't know if... why I was rebelling. At the time I felt very justified. Not now of course."

"So eventually you quit rock and roll, repaid your debts. I bet you've paid for every wrecked hotel room. You did *t'shuvah,* sought forgiveness, made restitution and went home. And, you became a rabbi, too."

"You make it sound so simple." He sighed. "Anyway, I didn't go home right away. First I had to deal with my family issues. I had to write it out. So I wrote…

He was staring at her, those bright blue eyes drilling into her. She'd thought she wouldn't commit herself to anything about this man, but suddenly she knew.

"You wrote, *The Prodigal.* I loved it; opera or musical, whatever." The critics all said *The Prodigal* straddled or joined those two categories. It had been on Broadway and had toured while Marnie was in rabbinical seminary.

"I wrote *The Prodigal,*" Eli agreed. "You are a very smart girl."

"Hardly," Marnie protested. "You practically handed it to me; all the business about your family; and combined with music."

"Every word true," he said emphatically. He put his wallet back in his pocket, but left his all-important picture on the table between them.

"But the author of *The Prodigal* wasn't Rabbi Eli Altman, or even the lead singer of SerpentSity. There was some name they used. And all the imagery, the whole story, is so…so…Christian," Marnie said. "We had long talks about it at seminary. How it was like *Godspell,* and *Jesus Christ Superstar,* and even *Joseph and the Technicolor Dream Coat.* We said someone ought to write a really Jewish rock opera, there's lots of great material out there, maybe one of the prophets. Nobody ever said the author was Jewish. He was known to be…

"Reclusive," Eli supplied the word. "He was known not to allow his picture to be taken full face. It was the period of time when I wanted it both ways. I wouldn't let them say the lead singer of SerpentSity had written *The Prodigal*. They just used this name I'd given them, Jesse Star.

"Jesse Star sounds totally phony,' Marnie said.

"It was meant to," he agreed readily.

'You like to hide in plain sight, like with your snake make up. It all disguises," Marnie said, tapping gently on his photo on the table between them.

"Yes," he said, "I'd used the name Jesse Star for years, although no one ever printed it very much. They just referred to me as Rattler when I was with SerpentSity, which was fine with me. Jesse Star was for when I needed a real name. It was obviously made up, a stage name."

"Sounds like you deliberately confused people."

"I obfuscated like crazy. By the time *The Prodigal* debuted I was reuniting with my family. I was going to *shul* on Saturday morning, going to the theater Saturday night, meeting with my folks, paying my debts, getting ordained, all of it, just like you said."

"Hardly a bad thing."

"It should have been harder," Eli said, looking down at the table. "SerpentSity had made me rich, but I'd blown so much of it, done enough coke to bankrupt even a rock star."

He would not look up at her so he didn't see the repulsion shivering through her at the thought of this man snorting or injecting cocaine.

"Then *The Prodigal* made me rich all over again."

"I'm not surprised," she said. "It's wonderful. It spoke to me. I mean everyone has family issues." She broke off, thankful they were concentrating on his issues right now.

He smiled at the idea she liked his opera, but she already knew he really listened. He'd remember what she'd said about her family and would want to know more about it. How would she ever tell him about Shalom?

"It should have been much, much harder," Eli repeated. "It made me rich, very rich. To this day the cast album, the rights, all of it, continues to make me very rich. *The Prodigal* has been declared a classic. Right now, somewhere in the world, high school seniors, leads in regional theater, are starring in *The Prodigal* and I'm getting paid. It's a classic, and I didn't even have to die."

"Why do you feel so bad? It isn't a crime to be successful. Is it because you've never been able to write…"

"Write another one? No, it's not that. I've never even tried. Right after *The Prodigal,* I went back to my family. I'm a Jewish prodigal. I went home. I went to the Conservative seminary. I was ordained."

"And?"

"Then, when I got here, I thought it was time to get married. After all, I'm almost thirty-seven."

Just a few years older than I, Marnie thought. Somewhere deep inside Marnie a small voice, said, 'A fellow rabbi, someone who had a big problem, with a secret in his past, the right age.' She was determined not to listen to the little voice. Those voices were not reliable. Marriage had been a trap.

"The reason I'm sitting here today, spying on those two" – a shrug of Eli's shoulder's indicated he meant

Sammy and Liora. "It started a year ago when I decided to get married."

"Things didn't work out?" Marnie said.

"No. Not at all. Things bombed." Eli shook his head in the negative so strongly his light blue *kippah*, his skullcap, threatened to slide off his head. He grabbed at it.

'Maybe it's his mother who made the *kippah* to match his shirt or his eyes,' said that untrustworthy little voice in Marnie's head.

"Why did you need to get married in the Mea Shearim orthodox community?" she said out loud. "You're not that kind of orthodox. You just said you were ordained Conservative. You want men and women to study text together. That's very liberal." Marnie said, making little quotation marks in the air meant to surround the words *Conservative* and *Liberal.*

Marnie and Tovah, many rabbis, spent a lot time on the subject of the dividing lines in Judaism; labels and practices. Years before, Tovah had moved from Reform to Conservative. Marnie, also ordained Reform, knew she was much more observant in her personal practices, but she'd never had to label her Judaism, since she didn't have a congregation to worry about.

"Given my history with girls, you can understand I didn't feel competent to pick out a wife on my own."

"So, you went to a *shatchan*," Marnie guessed. "You decided to get a professional matchmaker to pick out a nice little bride, one not despoiled by modern life."

There was more than a slight bitter edge to her comment. Eli looked up, embarrassed again, his face red.

She knew she had also flushed, but she wouldn't admit to it, wouldn't put up her hand to her face to feel the heat. She wouldn't look away either. She kept her eyes on his face. Let him blink first.

"Marnie," he said gently, and he did look down first, stirring what was left of his drink with a long straw. He put the straw down and reached out a hand to her, touched her arm, then withdrew his hand, as though he'd overreached.

"I couldn't make it up to all the groupies I'd...I'd known over the years. I thought I could at least try to meet the girl, the woman, I'd marry, in an ethical way."

Okay," Marnie agreed. "At its best using a *shatchan* is ethical, but..."

"But in the hands of a crook, it's a racket."

They looked at each other. "The father of those kids who walked down the street a few minutes ago was the *shatchan,* the crook. Marriages and engagements are his racket."

Marnie didn't directly acknowledge Eli's comment. How could she admit she had any connection to Shalom, the crook Eli was talking about? But then, despite an overwhelming sense of embarrassment, she knew she had to tell him about her background, her early marriage. Maybe just before she left Israel, she could tell Eli the truth?

He was watching her. It was definitely her turn. And, what was going to be gained by waiting? He had trusted her, without knowing much about her. Were they building something here?

You've never told anyone, she said to herself. Maybe this is where you start? This seems very important; different from anything before.

So, surprising herself, but feeling she was directed to tell, this was the moment for disclosure. Before 'this' went any further. Carefully she didn't ask herself what 'this' was, or might become.

She sensed Eli had to know her secrets, just as she knew his story. Even if it made no sense, they needed to be equal.

She reached into her shoulder bag, digging down to the bottom. Finally, finding and opening her wallet, she pulled a tiny photo in a plastic sleeve from a deep recess.

"It's my turn," she acknowledged and watched him nod in agreement. "We've got something in common. Here's my exhibit A."

She put her own photo down on the table; face up, next to the one Eli had left there. Marnie's picture had been cut from a larger snapshot. A smiling young woman, her head wrapped in a hair covering, the *tichel,* of the very observant, and wearing huge plastic-framed glasses, smiled up at them; a much younger Marnie. The children in front of her were clearly the two young Gasiths, Liora and Sammy.

"Rattler, or Jesse Star, or Rabbi Eli Altman, as you must now prefer to be called, meet Malka Gasith."

"Gasith is not a good name," Eli said, glancing quickly at Marnie's picture, then meeting her eyes once more.

"In fact, it's a very bad name."

"I agree with you," Marnie said. "But for some years, maybe some of the same years you were with SerpentSity, I was married to Shalom Gasith, and these two," Marnie tapped one finger on her snapshot. "These two were my stepchildren."

There was a look on Eli's face, so hurtful Marnie instantly regretted what she'd just tried to do. Who said honesty was the best policy? If this man couldn't understand, no one could. Hastily she stood up, grabbed her shoulder bag and her picture and almost ran down the street toward the corner where she'd be able to find a cab.

Eli was right behind her, reaching her in two long strides, grabbing her around her right wrist. "No, don't go," he said, sounding as desperate as she felt.

She couldn't believe the look that had been on his face. Eli Altman, aka Rattler, the rock star, the coke addict, the wrecker of hotel rooms and women's lives, had actually looked embarrassed for her.

For a moment she'd agreed, as though something as horrible as her marriage had been was her fault; that she'd caused some kind of irreparable damage.

"I didn't…," she said, and, "You didn't…," he said, simultaneously. They had both stopped, standing on the cobblestone road, his hand tightly around her wrist.

"He's the one…" he said, and, "He was the one…" she said, again, simultaneously. Silence again. It was the hottest part of the day. The early afternoon sun beat down on her head and radiated off the stone walls and heavily gated courtyards, the only visible part of houses on the street. Israel presented so many faces, from modern, urban architecture and wide freeways in other parts of the county, to the oldest parts of some of the cities.

As they stood there, one odd thought occurred to Marnie. Unless Eli had armed himself with some of that 50-count sun block he'd offered her yesterday, his fair skin would blister. She didn't want that to happen.

Eli spoke first, much to Marnie's relief. He was backing up toward the café, moving her along with him. "I'm sorry if I even looked like I blamed you. I know you must have been a victim, too, not the cause of anything. Come back. We're not finished here. Please come back."

He could probably feel the taut muscles in her arm, fighting the suggestion they sit down again.

"We need to get out of the sun," Eli said. "I burn badly. You probably do too. You're pretty fair and not tanned at all, even if you come from California."

Marnie found herself back in the same metal and plastic café chair. Eli stood above them, tilting the sun umbrella to a better angle, moving his chair around, closer to hers, so they were both in the shade. It gave her a few precious seconds to collect herself.

"It's taken me years to believe it wasn't my fault." she said, picking up on his last comment. It seemed very important to make him understand.

"I believe it most of the time. It's an old story by now. At least I thought it was. But recently Shalom showed up in L.A. Even now, I have a feeling it isn't nearly as interesting as your story. I met Shalom when I came to Israel the first time. I was newly in love with Jewish texts. I had just discovered both Torah and Talmud. I had just learned Hebrew. I was nineteen. At first he told me he was twenty-five. I believed him then; although eventually it was obvious he was over thirty."

"He wanted to get married right away," Eli guessed. He must have gestured to the café owner, because a bottle of cold water and another iced coffee was placed on the table in front of her.

"He was in a rush," she admitted. "He said the children needed me. He had custody of both of them, so I thought he must be an exceptional parent. I didn't know about negotiating a *get* and using your children as pawns to win custody, or money."

Eli made a rude noise in the back of his throat, but his eyes never moved from Marnie's face.

"I should have wondered why he'd been married twice, I guess. But he said *frum* men were married off so young, there were bound to be mistakes. I can't honestly tell you what I was thinking. It was my father who made us wait a little; a couple of months. To make sure we waited, my father let Shalom bring his own rabbi from Israel to Santa Barbara. My mother insisted on making a real wedding. It all took time. It cost my dad a fortune. Just three years later it cost him a fortune to extricate me, $20,000 for the *get.*" She looked ruefully at Eli. She also looked around as though she wasn't clear on how she'd been maneuvered back to the same spot at the café. Oddly, she felt quite safe again.

"You were his third wife," Eli said.

"Yes, I was. I guess getting married is how he makes a chunk of money from time to time."

"Right. He makes his personal fortune that way; the big bucks. Getting married –- and divorced of course – from time to time. For others, for clients, it's a much quicker, high volume operation. For others, he's into mass production."

"Mass…how can he…what do you mean…?" Marnie stuttered.

"He's got colleagues to work with of course. And, now he's using his kids," Eli said, tight-lipped. He slumped back in the small chair. "He makes his money from the people he gets them involved with. We would call it child abuse in the States, except I think he has their cooperation. Everybody ends up paying him. If it's not for a *get*, there's always something, a broken engagement, injury or suffering when his child is turned down, or turns someone down. He always figures out something, somebody else always pays. Never him."

"Are those activities why you called him a gangster?"

"You were one of his victims. If he's doing it all the time, it's a scam. He's a gangster, a hoodlum, a crook," Eli insisted, although he flushed, as though embarrassed for her again.

"It cost me to divorce Shalom," she admitted. "It's not unusual for the man to demand money for a *get*. I guess you could call it a scam, but how..."

"You're wondering how can you make a man pay?" Eli asked.

Marnie nodded, her head whirling. Had Shalom blackmailed the one-time leader of SerpentSity, or had he refused to let his daughter marry Eli, once he knew he was an ex-rock star? What else could it be? She recalled what she had said to Shalom, "You think of marriage as a way to pay off your bills." She'd been more correct than she knew.

Suddenly she was, again, very angry with Eli. She stood up again.

"Look, I promised Tovah I'd get back for the conference opening." Eli looked up at her, clearly surprised she wanted to leave again.

He reached out to her, but this time she pulled away and started walking. Then she spun around. "How could you even think of marrying a fifteen-year-old?" she flared.

He was already up and following after her. "Wait, I'll drive you back. I have to be at the King David too. And, you're right, of course. Except I didn't know she was fifteen. Actually, she was nearly fifteen and they said she was even older."

Marnie paused, and Eli took a minute to run back to their table, pulling his wallet out of his pocket as he went. Once there he peeled off what appeared to Marnie to be an outrageous number of colorful Israeli *sh'kelim.*

"Rent for the table," he said. He picked up his picture, and turned, walking quickly until he'd caught up to her again. Why had she waited for him?

"Look, my car is this way," he said, taking her wrist again. Then he dropped it. "Shouldn't touch you in Mea Shearim. Certainly not unless you want me to," he said.

But, he didn't ask if she wanted him to, just kept walking. If he was trying to keep the moment light it wasn't working.

"Do you really think I'd marry a kid?" What she thought actually seemed to matter.

"I would never have married her. Or, I realized, anyone else. Not under their system. A lot of things ended it for me, but especially her age, once I knew it. Anyway, you know your ex is plenty smart. He didn't particularly want us to get married. He wanted money instead of a marriage"

Then he added ruefully, "He got what he wanted, and while he was plenty smart, I was plenty dumb."

It was Marnie's turn to wince. Her ex. How could she ever have entered into a marriage with Shalom?

"Here's one way he does it." As they walked along Eli snagged a small local 'throw away' newspaper from a flimsy open rack. "Here's exhibit A," he said.

Quickly he leafed through it. They had turned a corner into a street so narrow it was hard to believe it was possible to park a car there. Eli waved the small newspaper in front of Marnie's face. "See, ads for potential brides and grooms, like personals back home.

"In these pictures and ads, every girl is gorgeous, and every man handsome." Was the loathing in Eli's voice for Shalom, or for himself?

"First there are the pictures, carefully doctored. No one looks their age. If they're older, they look younger. And, if they are fifteen, or even fourteen, they look older. The descriptions are just lies, nothing more. And it's on-line too, although that's just starting.

"According to Liora's ad she was eighteen, almost nineteen"

"Eighteen is hardly old enough...."

"I know, I know," he said, clearly embarrassed, "But if a girl is a lot older in this part of the *frum* world and still unmarried, it means something is wrong. Or they haven't been *frum* very long."

Marnie flushed. She was a lot older. And not *frum*. The way he spoke to her, as a colleague, was flattering, but it probably meant he wouldn't consider her anything but another rabbi. The only other important fact to Eli was she couldn't have been one of his groupies.

Eli seemed to understand at least part of what she was thinking. "Not you. You're not part of this world."

"Don't worry," Marnie said. "I'm certainly not willing to get married in this world again."

"Me either," Eli said, amazingly deep emotion in those two short words.

They were still walking, a very uphill climb. Marnie stopped in the middle of the road.

"But you didn't get married." She had to persist, even though this was one of the most embarrassing and, at the same time, one of the most intimate conversations she'd ever had with anyone. Thankfully Eli indicated they were only a step from his car, a tiny white Fiat.

"No, we didn't get married, but it took me more than three meetings with Liora to figure out what was up. By then…"

"By then she let you know she considered you two were engaged. The magic three dates and you're both taken." Marnie knew something about this.

When she'd met Shalom she couldn't believe they needed to know they were serious in three dates, three very public dates, or they had to break it off. There was no law about how many dates, but a strong custom had sprung up.

"So, suddenly, we were engaged, or at least promised. I actually saw her four times."

"And when you didn't want to go through with the marriage…" Marnie knew what was coming. She felt a little ill at the thought. "A girl who has been promised and doesn't get married, it's almost the same as a marriage. She'd be ruined."

"I had to almost divorce her. We actually needed a document, a kind of *get*. You're promised to a girl and you back out. In cases like this, believe me, the guy pays. Being threatened by Shalom and his cohort, you pay. I could afford it, but damn. I tried to do the right thing and I got nailed anyway. Then I find out from some reputable *shatchan* that I'm being scammed. Although how are you supposed to know who is reputable…"

"You found out Shalom has done this before," Marnie said.

"He's been selling Liora – not to characterize it even more baldly, but he's been selling her – since she was thirteen. He was claiming she was sixteen then, a young virgin bride; perfect for eighteen year old *Yeshiva* students.

"There are parents who want their sons married that young. And, if the boy is ready for *Kollel*, you can't attend unless you're married. So, you get married. Usually it works out. It's not a bad system in many ways. The two have common goals and all that. Shalom plays on that.

"But with him, some problem always arises. He'd pick some guy who was newly *frum,* who didn't really know the ropes, or who had parents willing to bank-role a marriage. Americans are his favorites, but there are South Africans and Australians. Always English speakers; *Anglo-Saxonim,* as the Israelis call native English speakers. I think that allows him to claim language-based confusions, even though he's from South Africa, too."

"He is," Marnie agreed, "but he claims he only spoke Afrikaans there." She shrugged.

Eli matched her shrug, both of them saying, in effect, "What can you do with a crook?"

"Once I knew what was going on, I thought someone had to stop him, so I went to the house," Eli explained. "I managed to get him outside…. I sort of…," Eli's voice trailed off. He looked down at his right hand, now fisted. His ears were red; his eyes unable to meet hers.

"What did you do?" Marnie said softly.

"I kind of took a poke at him."

"Kind of?" The fading bruise on Shalom's face came back to her.

"You scared him; he left the country."

"I don't think anything scares him. He was going to call the cops on me. For a country often at war they're very opposed to one-on-one violence in Israel."

Eli managed a smile. A possible police charge bothered him, probably reminding him of his past as part of SerpentSity. Slugging Shalom didn't actually seem to be a problem.

"But he was leaving the country anyway, so he went. He's getting married again, and it's in the U.S.," Eli said.

"In California," Marnie guessed.

"No, I don't think so," Eli said. "Somewhere in the Midwest, I believe. A very wealthy girl, newly observant."

Marnie found herself blushing furiously and, just like Eli, her hands were clenched into fists. Sitting there, sandwiched into Eli's tiny car she was suddenly very tired, even a bit dizzy. Too much had happened in a very short time. At least it felt that way.

Rabbi Eli Altman was making a huge impact on her life. How could it be? No man since Shalom had done that. Shalom had been a huge mistake. She would never allow anything like that to happen again.

But, she didn't want to stop whatever was going on right now. She wasn't certain what it was all about. After all, even though she had taken a twenty-hour flight to Israel, she'd only gone as far as a cafe on a sunny corner. But she was in Mea Shearim again.

"You shouldn't feel bad. It isn't your fault," Eli said.

"This will be Number five for him. He was married to someone after me, an Israeli. He actually sent me a note about it. I didn't respond.

"Number four didn't seem to present any problems. Something stopped him on this latest effort though," Marnie said thoughtfully. "He came to the States to get married, finds out he can't for some reason, and then comes looking for me in California."

"Did he hurt you?" Eli sounded heated, as though he'd slug Shalom again, any time he had a chance, but especially if he'd hurt her. Apparently, along with a confidante, Marnie had acquired a protector.

"No, he just scared me," Marnie said. "So I ran. I came here"

"This rabbis' conference," Eli said.

"It was my out, but I couldn't even tell them the truth at the *Yeshiva*, in case someone there told Shalom. I mean, I told them it was a conference, but not where it was being held. The doings of a Reform woman rabbi is not a big topic at Turov, believe me. And, I have to tell you: Tovah knows nothing about Shalom, or my marriage. Please don't say anything to her or anyone else."

"I wouldn't think of it, but thanks for letting me know. How did you ever keep it secret? And, why? It's a lot to carry around for a dozen years," Eli said.

"I was…it's a combination of being afraid and embarrassed, I think. Mostly the latter. I'm supposed to be able to figure things out," she said. "I think that was mostly why. Maybe."

"You mean being a genius academically was supposed to protect you? Whatever gave you such an idea? There you were what, nineteen, probably going on twelve. Years out of your depth socially. Your parents should have put their foot down and stopped you."

"You mean like your parents stopped you?" Marnie said.

Eli had the grace to blush. "I suppose you've got a point there," he admitted. "Boy when we mess up, we really do it.

"If I had Shalom here I'd slug him again, happily. For me, and for you. He shouldn't be able to frighten you. Although I'm glad you came here. Very glad."

He stopped speaking then, concentrating on the road. He turned and smiled at Marnie. "More later," he promised.

By now they'd left the ancient-looking part of Jerusalem for the groomed, suburban area around the King David Hotel. Eli concentrated on turning his Fiat into the driveway of the hotel.

When they entered the hotel, Marnie still felt as though she'd been away for days, not hours.

Tovah was standing in the lobby talking to the concierge.

"Oh good, you made it," Tovah said. "You're in plenty of time for the keynote."

"Keynote," Marnie repeated. She felt as though she'd never heard the word before.

"Rabbi Avrum Altman, the noted educator of men and women in the near-orthodox community. He's orthodox, or at least very traditional, but he teaches both sexes text, together. He's considered very radical but he's a great model, and a potential ally, for us."

Marnie turned around to look at Eli. "Altman?" she said, the name a question.

Eli reached around Marnie and shook hands with Tovah. 'You must be Rabbi Feldner," Eli said, "Marnie's friend. She's mentioned you more than once. Avrum Altman is my father. He does one hell of a speech. It's a subject he's passionate about. He knows your father, of course."

Marnie knew this sort of thing happened all the time in the relatively small rabbinical world. Who you knew made up a sort of informal game called Jewish Geography. How many connections do two people meeting for the first time actually have?

"I got your father's name from my father," Tovah confirmed. He's very impressed with what you're doing here. You have the brand new *Yeshiva*. Totally family-funded I understand. Very commendable."

"Well, we're a big family," Eli said.

"Then you are the son who is here working directly with him, the youngest. I'm the youngest in my family too," Tovah said.

Marnie just listened. If she had really listened before, as Tovah planned this conference, she'd already know all this. She looked at Eli with greater respect. He might be a wimp about how he'd tried to get married, but she had the feeling that 'family' funded meant Eli.

"We were so happy to get him as our keynote," Tovah said. "His views on men and women being educated together are revolutionary for any branch of traditional Judaism. It's okay in most of the Conservative movement of course, with women rabbis and so on."

Eli smiled at Tovah. "As a family we pride ourselves on being liberal. My *smicha*, ordination, is Conservative from JTS. That makes me the authentic family liberal. Most of my brothers were ordained at Yeshiva University, orthodox, of course. But, Yeshiva University likes to see itself as modern and engaged."

JTS was the major seminary of the Conservative movement of Judaism, the most traditional group allowing women to be ordained rabbis.

"How many brothers do you have?" Tovah asked. Eli and Tovah, with their father-rabbis and their web of connections in the Jewish community could play a particularly high stakes version of Jewish Geography. Both of them would be winners, Marnie figured. She didn't have the background for the game. Her parents had never interacted with the organized Jewish community. Her mother sometimes said that Marnie, along with her friends like Tovah, were the only real Jews she knew. Beatrice Holland didn't count her own Jewish friends, or herself, as 'real' Jews. Being Jewish was only a cultural marker for her, probably influencing the slang she used, what she ate and how she voted.

At the moment, besides listening to the idle specula-tions going on between Tovah and Eli, Marnie found she didn't mind just standing there. Her mind didn't seem to be working all that well.

"I'm one of seven; four boys, three girls," Eli said.

"You beat me," Tovah said, I've got five brothers, but I'm the only girl. I'm also the only rabbi. Hardly gets me on the map."

Somewhere at the back of Marnie's brain the idea that maybe one of Eli's sisters, or his mother, had made his *kippah*, jangled pleasantly.

Eli and Tovah were chatting about siblings, and both being the youngest in a large family, when the room suddenly seemed to shift around Marnie. She grabbed the closest stable object, Eli Altman's arm, because her knees seemed to have forgotten their function. Eli imme-diately grabbed her around the waist.

"Marnie, what's wrong?" Tovah said. The elegant foyer of the King David Hotel, Egyptian-themed, with those stunning columns in blue, gold and shining white, went grey in Marnie's eyes. It occurred to her, as her ears buzzed and the back of her neck grew cold; she might faint.

"I think I know what the problem is," Eli said. "We spent a lot of time out in the heat of the day, didn't eat much, drank way too much really strong coffee and talked too much. Let me get her upstairs and get some food into her. If we don't make the speech, don't be surprised," he said to Tovah. "It's a great speech, but I've heard it before, so I can give Marnie the highlights if I have to."

Somewhere in Marnie's mind, half functioning though it was, she noted Tovah stepped aside to let Eli carry out his plan for her without argument or discussion. Tovah willing to let someone take over her friend's life was easily one of the most amazing things Marnie had ever seen.

CHAPTER ELEVEN

The conference was in full swing the next morning. Tovah was up and out early while Marnie slept until well past eight a.m. There was a note for her on Tovah's bed:

Marnie, here's your registration material. If your tall redhead wants to take up more of your time, go ahead. One speaker today might interest you. There's a woman Talmud scholar appearing at four this afternoon, just before dinner. You might also be interested in the Judaica display. There's lots of stuff to buy, plus stuff that can be custom-made: even egalitarian Ketubot, marriage certificates. Maybe one day you'll need one.

'Your redhead.' And 'maybe one day you'll need one.' Honestly, Tovah was about as subtle as a tank. She had no sense of proportion. Eli had just been kind last night. They had gone up to her room and while she washed up and then rested, Eli ordered a meal from room service.

While they had waited for dinner, he'd read *Ha'aretz,* the daily Hebrew-language paper. He'd been a perfect gentleman.

By the time they'd eaten, Marnie was reasonably well recovered, so they had gone down to hear the last part of Eli's father's speech. Later they'd looked through the Judaica display too; even the marriage certificates, designed to prevent men from holding all the power in a divorce.

Marnie hadn't said a word about her *get* of course. Nothing would have brought Shalom into line. Her only comment was to ask Tovah, "Do you suppose men who sign these take them seriously. Could they be binding?"

"I suppose it's like anything else," Tovah said. "Depends on who marries you. But for us, for Conservative rabbis, they damn well better be binding."

Eli had nodded, leaning in close to read the traditional Aramaic of the marriage contract, the added clauses and the English translations. "Looks legal to me." He said. "But I suppose they'll be cases brought before a million religious courts before anything really changes."

Good for him, Marnie thought. She agreed with him. It would take a while for real change. Maybe the two of them were destined to be friends. Maybe she'd visit Israel again and actually teach a class at his new *Yeshiva*. Or, maybe he'd visit California or found another a branch of his school. L.A. was big enough for an alternative *Yeshiva*.

She was as bad as Tovah. Eli had been kind and considerate. One gallant gesture didn't make them partners for life. As she thought about it, it probably meant quite the opposite. He had no interest in her at all. The trauma that Shalom had inflicted on him probably turned him off marriage forever. Were they both the same in that way?

The phone rang.

"Good morning," Eli said. "I hope I didn't wake you."

Marnie sat up as though the phone in her hand had pulled her upright. "No, of course you didn't wake me. I was just going through the conference material to select..."

"Tovah told me there's lots of Israel you've never seen. I have to drive to Tel Aviv today, a short trip. It'll probably barely register since you're used to traffic in L.A., maybe an hour in each direction. Why don't you come along?"

Marnie tried to think of some good, substantial reason to refuse the trip. "The conference, there's a speaker," she said weakly She wanted to go with Eli. That must mean it was a bad idea.

"I'll have you back in plenty of time to catch the woman Talmud teacher. Tovah thought you'd want to hear what she has to say.

"We can have lunch on the beach. You'll feel like you're in Santa Barbara. Fresh fish; tilapia. They call it St. Peter's fish here."

"I left Santa Barbara, if you recall." Marnie had to laugh.

"So, you'll enjoy the nostalgia."

Marnie had the distinct feeling her life had just been taken over by Eli, ably assisted by Tovah. She would never be able to stand up against such a combination. Maybe she didn't want to resist?

Eli went right on planning. "And, you wanted to talk to Shalom's kids. I think we ought to start with Liora. I know where she works. We ought to see her tonight, tomorrow at the latest. Whatever you're going to do, it should be right away. What if Shalom comes back?"

Marnie couldn't believe it. Her cause had become his.

"Okay," she said. "Tel Aviv will be great."

"Tel Aviv is a hole, really. Much too American, and the weather isn't great. It's very humid. But it's where the music scene is and most of the business world. Eat some breakfast this time. You don't want to be one of those tourists always fainting. I'll have water in the car, so don't worry about that. Forty-five minutes, okay?"

"Okay," Marnie agreed. She would order some breakfast, grab a shower, get dressed and be ready to go on time.

She had no idea of exactly where this was going; with the two of them. Except to Tel Aviv at this moment.

She couldn't even talk to Tovah about it, because her normally sensible friend had actually mentioned love at first sight yesterday. That was just silly, wasn't it?

Lunch on a Mediterranean beach, at a restaurant where you sat with your feet in the sand and were served fish grilled over an open flame, did feel a little like Santa Barbara. But, the energy of Tel Aviv was more like New York than California.

It was hard to believe that Israel was so small you could get from Jerusalem to Tel Aviv and back in less than a day. The one-way trip was longer than the hour Eli had predicted and when Marnie pointed that out, she really felt at home, since he said, "It all depends on the traffic, you know."

Besides lunch, the day included running two of Eli's errands. It would usually have taken Marnie longer to drive to her parents' home in Santa Barbara from Los Angeles then to go from Jerusalem to Tel Aviv. Mind you, while the traffic would have been even worse, the drivers would have been less terrifying.

It was three forty-five when Eli pulled into the parking area of the King David. The valet parking foreman looked surprised when the two of them, Eli six foot four and Marnie, almost six foot, unfolded themselves from Eli's miniscule white Fiat. Like those clowns in the little car at the circus. But, looking slightly ridiculous didn't really bother her just then.

"I might as well listen to the lady on Talmud," Eli said. "It'll help me figure you out." He grinned.

Eli seemed quite content to tag along and hear what the woman who taught Talmud had to say. The most important message in her speech seemed to be that others in her position should avoid 'undignified' circumstances. Would this speaker think a cubicle with a window undignified, Marnie wondered?

She could have given this lecture herself, complete with a slide show: how she taught Talmud at the University of Judaism, to mixed classes, casually dressed, with students ranging from bright teenagers to grandfathers and grandmothers who audited her class.

She could also show everyone what it was like to teach at Turov. She could give a fully illustrated lecture: her boys lining up and exiting the room in front of the special window of her little cubicle. All the hardware and the computer she had that controlled her classroom, and especially her cubicle.

If this group of her colleagues, women rabbis of the last decade, saw what she saw every day, would they be able to figure out how these two groups of people, liberal Jews and orthodox Jews could continue to talk to each other, or would their worlds continue to diverge?

No one in the audience asked about a woman teaching orthodox boys – or even orthodox girls – come to think of it. She knew that many of her Reform colleagues considered teaching in the orthodox community a waste of time. They'd let her know that. Of course most of them would never be invited to teach there anyway. Was Marnie the only one trying to straddle those two worlds?

Listening to the lecture, Marnie considered raising any number of questions, but finally decided all she would precipitate would be an argument. That would be undignified.

Eli had said, "I like your thinking. Why you teach at Turov." For the moment that was enough for her.

After an early dinner with Eli – they'd shared two of their three meals that day – the two of them left the King David Hotel to confront Liora at the day care center – the *gan* – where she worked part time. They drove to The German Colony where the *gan* was located.

The German Colony was an older, affluent, residential area of the city, one of the earliest built outside the walls of the Old City. It had been settled even before the State of Israel existed. Most people lived in two or three story apartment buildings with wide windows and many balconies. The foliage was lush; philodendrons tall enough to touch the eaves of houses and leggy poinsettias so ungainly they didn't suggest Christmas, even to North Americans.

As they drove, Marnie's level of tension escalated so much she could hardly breathe. She and Eli had talked about her 'plan' for confronting Liora, but in the end Marnie had no idea what she would say. The only thing the two of them agreed on was Eli would have to stay hidden, parking his car around the corner.

Liora worked late in the day, so they went to the school right after dinner.

"If you talk to her, the relationship you had might still call up some kind of loyalty. Were you in touch after you left Israel?" Eli asked.

"I wrote to both children for two or three years after I left. The whole year I was in Israel I actually mailed the letters home and my parents forwarded them to Israel, so Shalom would see they came from California."

Marnie remembered choosing and mailing toys and clothes, wondering if they would ever get to Liora or Sammy.

"The packages and letters went through for a while, then started to come back, marked 'refused.' I doubt the children ever saw more than one or two of them."

In early October it was still fairly light. Marnie waited outside the door of the *gan* as parents came to pick up their young children. One after another the older teachers left and finally, there was Liora, her back turned to Marnie in order to lock the regular door and the heavy security gate covering the regular door with strong mesh and steel bars.

"Liora," Marnie said; her voice shaky. The girl turned around. Close up Marnie could see how pretty she was; with a soft oval face and huge dark eyes. No wonder Shalom had little trouble finding men who wanted to marry his daughter. She could have been any age, Marnie realized, fifteen to thirty five. There was no recognition in Liora's eyes at first, but then she said in Hebrew. "You were with 'him' at the café."

The girl's face hardened, suddenly looking much older. It was as though the word 'him' had spikes on it. Those soft, dark brown eyes filled with anger – and fear too.

Eli had suggested Liora might run, so Marnie was ready. Before the girl had the key out of the deadbolt on the security door, she'd taken the girl's hand in hers. It was a friendly gesture, but it would also let Marnie restrain Liora if she tried to run.

Marnie was the one panicking. Liora stood staring at her. Marnie wondered how to hold this child here, to reach her in some way, to make the few minutes she would have really count.

"Liora, it's me, *Ima* Malka," Marnie said in Hebrew. She hadn't thought of the name the children had used for her, Mother Malka, in years. She loathed Shalom using the name Malka, but she had cherished the children's version. She hadn't consciously remembered it when she'd tried to rehearse what she was going to say to Liora, all the way back from Tel Aviv with Eli and on their way to the *gan*. No rehearsal would ever have yielded the totally instinctive words that had just popped out her mouth.

If she'd been looking for the words to keep Liora from fleeing, Marnie had said just the right thing. The girl's eyes grew even wider, the pupils dilated, and Marnie saw tears well up. Suddenly it was as though Liora were four again. Could this child remember enough of when Marnie was her mother to make her cry now?

"But you were with 'him,'" Liora repeated. Marnie had forgotten Liora's strong Israeli accent; with the almost British precision of consonants.

"I only met him there. I was waiting to see you and Sammy. I didn't even know you knew him." It was close enough to the truth, and Marnie certainly wasn't going to get into the possible role Liora might have in Shalom's marriage scams, willingly or unwillingly.

"You remember me," Marnie said to the girl, awe in her voice.

"Sammy and I, we talked about you a lot. I remember the talking, maybe more than you. I didn't remember you were so…so pretty," the girl said, blushing. "Or that you are so American."

"You are just as pretty now as you were then," Marnie said and was pleased to see Liora blush and look down. "Do you remember when I went away?" Marnie asked.

"*Abba* sent us to Auntie and Uncle in Beersheva, and when we came back he said you'd gone back to California because you wanted to go to school, and that wasn't allowed," Liora said.

"We didn't know what was true. We could go to school and be your children. But *Abba* said an *Ima* could not. He gave you a choice, and you chose school."

Liora looked like a student in her own *gan*, a very young child who had been told something making no sense. It just had to be accepted. The girl leaned back against the heavy grillwork covering the door. Then, suddenly, as though remembering something she'd been told she should always do, Liora stood up very straight.

"I only went when your father wouldn't let me see you anymore," Marnie started to explain. Then, with decision, she said. "Liora, never mind all the 'I said' and 'He said.' It's not important. Your father came to find me in California and…."

"And you ran away again, because you wouldn't tell him what he needs to know," the girl said. She didn't seem to make any judgment; just stated what she'd been told. There seemed to be little weight to her words. It was as though this girl expected behavior like this from everyone.

"Liora, it's much more complicated."

"I know. I know. But *Abba* wants to marry Katie, and her father won't let her marry, and you won't let him marry either."

"Katie?" Marnie asked.

"Katie is his…*bashert*…his fiancée. She lives in Indiana." Liora's strong Israeli accent made the location sound very exotic. Did she even know where Indiana was?

"Will you go to the wedding?"

"It is too much for all of us to fly," Liora explained. "And Sammy won't go, so it is better I stay here and look after the house…and Sammy."

"Does Sammy like Katie?"

"He likes her. Maybe he likes her too much. She is very young. Sammy says she is too young to marry *Abba*."

"And you agree with your *Abba,* or with Sammy?"

"I agree with *Shalom Bayit*," Liora said. Now there was real hostility in her voice. Peace in the home was the traditional concept Shalom had flung at Marnie every time they disagreed over something. It was a wife's duty – a woman's duty – in this case, a daughter's duty, to keep peace in the house. Had Shalom made Liora responsible for *Shalom Bayit* in his home, since she was the only female living there? That was too big a burden for a young girl.

Remembering the obscene gestures Liora had flung into Eli's face, and from the greater distance of the back of the bus, she was surprised Shalom could get Liora to do things she didn't want to do. But he'd had years to bend her to his will. Marnie couldn't face what Shalom might do to maintain control of his daughter, or any woman.

Liora, her face and voice now carefully neutral, said *"Abba* will marry whomever he wants to marry, like always. Except you won't let him, he said when he called. So, he's angry," the girl said, as though such anger were totally reasonable. Then she added, more curious than anything else, "How did you stop him from marrying Katie?"

"Your *Abba* is really marrying someone named Katie?" Marnie asked. She needed some time to think.

"When they get married her name will be *Chava,"* Liora said, very calm. Something about Liora's responses troubled Marnie. What could such acceptance, such a flat affect, mean?

The two of them had been standing in front of the *gan* for several minutes now. It seemed Liora was in no rush. She just stood there, as though Marnie had tacit permission to set the terms of their meeting. With an idle gesture, she swung her heavy set of keys back and forth, as though hypnotizing herself.

"He married Esther five or six years ago, and she lived with us almost four years before she left," Liora said. "You only stayed two years and a little bit." There was no hint of blame in Liora's voice, she was simply quoting facts.

"Abba thinks Katie, *Chava,* will stay longer."

"Did your *Abba* actually say why he can't marry *Chava?* He must be worried," Marnie said. Then she added the important question, the test, "And, when your *Abba* calls home, will you tell him you've talked to me?"

"What will you do if I say I'll tell him?" Liora wanted to know. Everything in her young life seemed to have been a trade-off.

"If you tell your *Abba* I'm here, I will have to go away, again," Marnie said. "I would hate to do it, because I want to know you better, as a grown up person."

"And, Sammy too?" Liora asked.

"Do you think Sammy wants to know me?"

Marnie's question made Liora pause. You could almost see her trying to think out the right answer, the answer Marnie wanted.

"Sammy is different now. For a while he's been different," Liora spoke very slowly. It was obviously very difficult for her to question anything her brother or father might do. But, they couldn't keep her from seeing and noting the changes.

Marnie waited. Liora seemed so repressed in all her answers to questions, despite her seeming willingness to do as others said she should, to accept anything that went on at home. But this was the same girl who had given Eli the finger. Obviously, not marrying him had upset her. And, just as obvious, Liora carried some steel deep within.

Liora didn't seem to question most things, or to try to assess them, except by the standard of whether her father or her brother thought it was good. But, in some personal matters she had her own ideas. Eli had been one of those ideas.

Marnie tried to think of how Liora would strike her if they'd just met. She remembered an articulate, questioning four year old. Certainly people didn't change all that much? Had Liora been ill? Had she been punished excessively? Marnie knew there was nothing wrong with her intellect. Someone had taught her it was best to do what those in authority wanted her to do.

Being orthodox didn't do this to most women. Most *frum* women were outspoken. They ran their homes like queens. Often they handled, and sometime earned, most of the money in a family. In Judaism they had different ritual obligations then men. But in the areas that were theirs, they reigned, never experiencing their lives and responsibilities as 'lesser' in any way.

But, Liora had grown up with several stepmothers and her father and brother. It had not been a normal household.

Eli was waiting around the corner in his car. He would have to wait. Marnie couldn't leave Liora right now and she knew that if the girl saw 'him,' – Liora had never used Eli's name – she would run off into the night and certainly tell Shalom or Sammy all about it.

"Sammy thinks *Abba* has been married enough times."

"He told your father that?" Marnie couldn't believe it.

"Not before, but he did when *Abba* called and said there was a problem. Then Sammy said, 'You've been married enough. You don't need to get married anymore.'"

"Why does Sammy say your *Abba* doesn't need to get married anymore?"

"I think Sammy said it because he will have so much money soon. I think that's what he means. Because he does so much work with computers. He's very smart about computers. So, Sammy thinks *Abba* didn't need a bride's dowry so much. But, if he finds his *bashert*, he should get married. Everyone should be married. I was going to get married before, when I was very young.

But the man wasn't good enough, *Abba* said, and even Sammy told me not to. Anyway it didn't work out. Then I met 'him.'"

"You mean Eli, the man I was sitting with in the café," Marnie asked.

"Yes. He is a *Rav,* some kind of a rabbi. He is handsome. Well, maybe not so handsome, but tall, and rich. But he wouldn't marry me. He was really mad about something. He and *Abba* even had a fight. Part of it was about me."

Liora looked hurt that Eli wouldn't marry her, but she also had the look of a teenager when two boys want to take her to the prom. That's the kind of thing she should be worrying about, Marnie thought. This girl is in no way ready to be married.

"*Abba* says he will find me someone else, but I'm afraid the next one will be old, or not learned, or something will be wrong with him, because 'he' would not marry me," Liora said. "Because 'he' wouldn't...."

The girl wouldn't say, 'because I've been ruined,' but she must be thinking that. Was she innocent, not understanding what her father and her brother were doing?

What Liora was saying frightened Marnie almost as much as the look in the girl's dark brown eyes. This young woman, so beautiful, could only imagine getting married. It was her only goal. But, there were options for her. There were excellent schools for orthodox young women. They could do interesting public service, since they couldn't serve in the military alongside men. There were seminaries and universities in the States and in Israel, catering to intelligent, young orthodox women. Marnie didn't even know how much education Liora had. High school had to be paid for in Israel, so Liora might have only finished eighth grade.

Shalom must be educating his children somewhat. From what Liora said, Sammy knew all about computers. Had he been taught, or just picked it up like American children often did, as though it were part of their lifeblood.

As for Liora, were Shalom and her brother Sammy willing to take advantage of her, or frighten her into her present behavior? If the Gasith men had an organized scheme about marriages or near-marriages as a money-making plan, it seemed unlikely that Liora was in on it.

"You know, I'd like to talk to Sammy too," Marnie said, half-baked ideas for solving this dilemma racing through her mind as she continued to observe Liora. Truthfully, she didn't think most of her plans would ever come to pass.

"But will Sammy tell your *Abba* if he knows I'm here?"

"Sammy will tell *Abba* whatever he wants to know. At least he always did before. Sammy and *Abba*, the two of them…they…they work…."

"They work at their marriage business together," Marnie guessed.

"Marriage-business," Liora said, seemingly confused by those two words coming together. What had Shalom and Sammy colluded in? What did they hide from Liora?

"You only think it is a business because you were with 'him.' He said that too," Liora said. "He said something like that. He came to the house and he hit *Abba*. That was very bad. It's more important to make *shidduchim,* matches, then just to make a business. It's *HaShem's* work on earth. God can't make all the marriages, so the

123

shatchans do it. They make matches to assist *HaShem,* the Holy Name. So, it's holy work."

Marnie would have to leave all those big ideas alone. She couldn't get into it with Liora, although it was useful to know how the girl thought. What an odd mixture of deference to authority and hostility she exhibited. She'd been willing to tweak Eli's nose, to give him the finger. But she also seemed like a frightened mouse.

What had a possible marriage meant to Liora? Well, at the moment Marnie wasn't going to get an answer to that question. The important thing, Marnie considered, was to stay in touch.

Liora seemed to sense what Marnie needed to know. *"Abba* won't come home unmarried. He said so. He's trying to figure out what is stopping things. Katie, I mean Chava's family, wouldn't have a wedding in Israel, a Jewish wedding. They want an American marriage. They insist on it. So, until he figures it out, *Abba* won't come back. Katie is mad at her family. She wants whatever *Abba* wants."

Somewhere at the back of Marnie's mind a small bell rang; something about her marriage to Shalom. But she had to ignore it. Whatever thought was rushing through her mind, she would have to retrieve it later. At the moment she had to concentrate on gaining Liora's trust.

"You won't tell him about me on the phone?" Marnie needed a promise from Liora, although she felt Sammy or Shalom could probably get this girl to change her mind about any promise if they really wanted to.

Well, she would have to risk it. Even if Shalom came back suddenly, he wasn't going to attack her. He needed his wedding, Jewish and American secular, more than he needed to dominate Marnie. That was clear. To him a secular marriage wasn't important, but, if it's what Katie's family wanted, it would have to be done.

Marnie stopped again. A thought… But the thought fled in the face of her need to reassure Liora. Marnie pulled out a business card and wrote her international cell phone number on the back.

She didn't give the girl her hotel room number or even the name of the hotel. Just in case Liora wanted to tell Sammy, or her father, she wouldn't be able to simply divulge the name of the hotel.

"If anything happens, you'll call me, right?" Marnie said.

Liora looked very doubtful. "When I go to the store in a day or two, I'll phone you." Liora was ready to make that promise; but nothing more. "I'll call you before *Shabbat*. Maybe, if I've talked to Sammy by then…."

But Liora stopped. An invitation for Shabbat would have been forthcoming from most women, but the circumstances that bound Liora and Marnie, and what separated them, years of history, multiple marriages, a broken engagement, the girl's inability to think beyond anything but her possible marriage, made such an invitation unlikely.

Marnie settled for the promise she had: Liora would call her. She had already decided. If she didn't hear from this girl by Shabbat, she would go back to Mea Shearim.

"Don't come to the house, though," Liora said, as though reading Marnie's mind. "Sammy won't like it. He's still very angry with you. Because you left him; you left us. He used to say you were the best, but lately he has only bad things to say about most people, even you."

"Liora, when I left, you were four, Sammy was not even eight. How can he still be mad?"

"It's not still mad," Liora tried to explain, as though she wanted to understand her brother herself. "It's new, and it has to do with his new business. Sammy has his own business now. With computers. *Abba* doesn't really understand computers. He's not sure Sammy's new business is good."

"What is Sammy doing with computers?" Marnie asked.

"I can't say. Some I don't know, and some I promised I wouldn't say." Liora admitted. "It's a service for those *chutz l'aratz;* for Jewish people living outside Israel."

"Some service for those in the Diaspora," Marnie said, wondering. But Liora was looking across the street to where a bus waited.

"We'll talk again soon," Marnie said. It's our secret, at least for a few days, right?"

Liora nodded agreement. "A secret," she agreed. "A secret from *Abba* and from Sammy. Is it a secret from 'him' too?"

"No. He had to know. I didn't know where you worked. And, we were together when we saw you. He told me what happened. How bad he felt for you and for himself. But, I won't tell him what you and I have said tonight."

Liora stared at Marnie. Was she regretting the promise she'd just given, since it involved 'him'? She probably could be as mercurial as any other teenager. Liora pulled her hand out of Marnie's grasp, turned and ran across the street to the bus waiting for her. Damn the good Israeli transport system. Liora jumped on the bus and sat down, looking straight ahead. A look so intense it could penetrate stone.

Marnie ran over to the bus. Liora's window was open. "Liora, honest, we'll settle all this. You'll be safe. We can get to know each other again. The *Rav* will help. We can be friends. He's a rabbi. You know that. I'm a rabbi too. You can trust us."

It was doubtful that any statement Marnie had made, except her declaration that she was a rabbi, would have caused Liora to look at her again. "A *Rav*? How can you be a *Rav*? Such things don't happen. And, if you're really a *Rav*, a *Rav* like him, what good does that do? *Abba* says even he is not the same, not really the same, not like a real *Rav*. Not 'him.' A real *Rav* wouldn't run around in blue jeans."

"An American rabbi would, outside Israel," Marnie said.

The bus pulled away, but, Marnie saw, Liora was looking right at her. Perhaps the girl was intrigued enough to keep her secrets. Marnie thought they would be able to speak again, at least once more. She didn't know how much more she could accomplish, but she thought Liora's curiosity, which seemed awakened a little, enough to confuse her, would bring her back to speak to her *Ima Malka* again. It would have to be before the authority of her father or her brother overwhelmed the girl again.

CHAPTER TWELVE

O nce the bus pulled out and disappeared around the corner on the way to Mea Shearim, Marnie walked back to where Eli had parked the Fiat. She would have to watch herself. She was very angry, at least with anyone male.

"Did Liora seem very repressed to you when you met with her?" she asked Eli.

"How would I know?" he said. "A talking monkey could go on those dates they set up for us. You go to a public place and you take turns asking each other questions. It's all scripted. When she knew I was a rabbi, that was wonderful, and the fact that my father was a well-known rabbi was great. Even not being really *frum*, was okay. She told me, she said it's a wife's pleasure to follow her husband's *minhagim,* his customs. She would be Jewish as I was Jewish. Maybe, just a little more orthodox. I would have to teach her my customs, she said. I'm surprised she didn't begin to take notes about how details are handled at *Chez* Altman.

"She liked that I was learned, that was important. The only way you really find out anything real about someone is to ask questions of the people you know in common. I didn't know anyone to ask about her, and she couldn't ask anyone about me."

"Did you ask her how much schooling she had? Did she go to high school?

"High school? Why would she not have gone to high school? She should still be in high school if she's only 16."

"Eli," Marnie didn't want to sound stern but she was so annoyed. "Think for a moment. She works for her dad in his store. Probably for nothing. You said she works at least three shifts a week at the gan, for very little, I'm sure. There's no time for school. And, you have to pay for high school here."

"But Sammy, her brother, he's some kind of computer *maven*. She told me so. He must have gone to school."

"Maybe school for a son, but not for a daughter? She only needs to be smart enough to go on dates that a trained monkey could manage. You just said so."

Marnie folded her arms across her chest and stared straight ahead, through the Fiat's windshield. Their conversation was fogging the glass. They should really leave before something stupid happened, before she said something she'd regret.

"She was prepared to marry you, you know. Shalom broke it up, but Liora doesn't know that," Marnie said.

"She doesn't understand what they're doing. The first time the man was old and not very attractive, so she was relieved not to marry him. But, if they'd insisted, she would have. I'm quite sure she didn't know then, and didn't know with you, that the whole thing was a scam. She's another victim, really.

"As for you, you should have asked some of these questions during at least one of those four dates. Can you multiply and divide? How far did you go in school? Did you study Hebrew, Yiddish, English? She speaks English, but she did when she was a child too, so that's not a surprise. All of Shalom's wives have been English speaking. You should have asked her at least where she studied."

Marnie was getting very wound up. In addition, there was something at the back of her brain; some little bell had rung while she was speaking to Liora. She couldn't quite remember though.

She swiveled as much as possible to look at Eli. "You should have taken some responsibility for what's been going on."

Eli countered, "Isn't the *shatchan* representing us supposed to know those things? I didn't know she was his daughter. I didn't think to ask...."

"You can't just hire someone to do a job for you, not something like getting married, and expect it to work out. You're not a talking monkey either. You should have asked," Marnie said.

Her voice was sharp. She turned away from him, fearful he would see how angry she was.

"Surely you had the major responsibility. What were you going to do if it didn't work out?" She felt compelled to turn back to him, to look Eli straight in the eye. How could he have bought into a system he didn't believe in, and didn't fully understand?

"What were you thinking about when you decided on using a *shatchan*?" she demanded.

"Look Marnie, you're probably right. I ought to have taken responsibility for whomever I'd marry and how I found her. I honestly thought, well, I don't know how honest it was, but it seemed like an easy way, and the right way. I live in fear of running into my groupies. Someday soon someone will write a book about all the time I was on the road, and whomever I'm married to will be very embarrassed. I figured if my wife lived totally outside the real world she'd be protected."

"You weren't trying to protect your would-be wife. You don't know anything about her. You were protecting yourself. You were prepared to marry someone really observant just to protect yourself. Somebody far more observant than you will ever want to be. You want women to learn with men and pray together. How could you marry someone who had no idea about that sort of egalitarianism?"

"No, I wanted to protect her, whoever she might be," Eli said, stubbornly, rejecting Marnie' thesis.

"You wanted to protect yourself," Marnie repeated. "You figured someone from this world might never hear about you and your background. She wouldn't even know what SerpentSity was."

Why was she giving Eli such a hard time? She had some idea why she was so disappointed in Eli, but she wasn't ready to deal with it at the moment

"I suppose I was," Eli said. "I suppose I was." His admission surprised her almost enough to make her want to cry. He started the Fiat and began to drive. Clearly he wasn't going back to the hotel. He was driving away from the center of town.

"Let's drive a little, to cool off," he said. "I can't leave things with you this way."

That took Marnie by surprise and, again, instead of being angry, it made her even sadder.

The damage people did to themselves was far worse than trashed hotel rooms. Marnie kept glancing over to Eli. He had directed the car out past the suburbs. It was late, very dark. The only other cars on the road were military patrols, who flashed their headlights into the Fiat before they let it pass. In one or two places war memorials stood by the roadside, where battles had taken place in 1948, in 1966. The memorials were not cairns, walls or statues. They were burned out tanks or gun emplacements left standing, with only a plaque added. These wrecked military emplacements were mementoes of war and death in this small country. Neither Marnie nor Eli commented.

As they rounded a bend that brought the city back into view Eli pulled into a look-out area, a flattened space in the bare brown hills that surrounded the city. They were high above the plateau of Jerusalem, looking down on the floodlit walls of the Old City and the brilliantly illuminated plaza in front of the Wailing Wall.

Marnie felt the trills of her nerves as they sat in the dark. Seeing Liora had left her feeling guilty; something she hoped Eli felt too.

The two of them, so tall, made the interior of the Fiat seem smaller than Marnie's MG, and much less comfortable. She hoped this tiny car at least got fabulous gas mileage.

Marnie found herself trying to imagine her next conversation with Liora. What could she say to her? What could she do for the girl? What would make a real difference in her life? What would she do about Shalom, and why, why, did he think he needed a divorce? Could this whole thing have only started a few days ago, when, desperate to escape Shalom, she chose to come to Israel for her class reunion? California seemed very far away right now.

Someone shook her arm.

"Boy," Eli said. "When you're thinking things through, there is no reaching you. What a level of concentration. Want to tell me what's on your mind? As long as it isn't more about me, the bad choices I've made."

Marnie shuddered and tried turning toward Eli, as much as was possible. "No, no, it isn't that. I'm all done with that. I'm even a little sorry about what I just said. I suppose you were taken in."

"Well, I'm grateful for that. I don't think I bear all the blame. I'm delighted we don't have to go another round."

Eli beeped the horn on his car, a tinny sound like the signal for another round in a boxing match.

The sound echoed in Marnie's brain. "I had a thought but I put it aside to talk to Liora. That bell, your car horn, all about my wedding to Shalom."

"What was different about it, you mean? I've been thinking about that too."

No one ever said that to Marnie. No one was ever thinking the same thing she was thinking.

Eli went on. "Your wedding was the only one of Shalom's marriages that took place in the States. That's the one big thing."

"And this wedding, the one Shalom is trying to pull off, it's at home too. In Indiana, Liora said."

"So, in that one regard it is like your wedding."

"Right, exactly. But the major thing about my wedding, what made it different, was my father. You can't underestimate his impact. He set up my wedding."

"Meaning your father is sneaky enough to have pulled off something?" Eli asked, with a big smile. How had she ever thought of this man as homely? He had such a strong face.

"No, my father is smart, but very low key. My mother is smart too, but she's much sneakier than my father."

Eli laughed so hard Marnie could only watch and marvel. If he laughed like this for much longer he'd be crying.

When Eli could finally speak, he was so out of breath his words were barely audible. "So, did you inherit your brains and sneakiness from one or the other, or from both?" Then he reached over and enveloped Marnie in an enormous hug. He didn't wait for an answer. "I just love you," he said. "No one else could have said something like that so seriously."

"I didn't mean… not that my mother… I get it from… I just thought I would tell you what… I'm not sure what I mean anymore," she admitted. "I've never been quite so…"

"Confused?"

"I guess confused would cover it," she agreed.

Eli had un-wrapped his long arms from around her and was grasping the upper part of each of her arms. His left elbow was bumping up against the windshield of the car. His right arm was now compressed awkwardly between his body and the car seat. The steering wheel had to be poking him in the ribs, even though his seat and Marnie's too, were pushed as far back as possible.

"I love you," Eli repeated, sounding just as amazed as Marnie felt at that moment.

Marnie felt her face freeze. She had no idea what to do, how to respond. How not to frighten him away; how to let him go on?

It turned out she didn't need to do anything. Eli pulled her closer to him. He didn't ask. He kissed her gently, forehead, cheek and finally, on the mouth. A real kiss. A kiss she responded to with the kind of desire she'd never felt before. She wanted to. She had to. Along with the kiss his hug seemed to include her whole body, even though only their upper bodies touched.

He finally pulled away. "Enough," Eli said, "Enough for now. We'll have to talk. But it's not something we have to talk about right now. Just don't forget," he said. He kissed her again. Marnie could only nod her head in agreement. She couldn't say a word, but she certainly wouldn't forget.

CHAPTER THIRTEEN

The next day it was Marnie who called Eli at six thirty a.m. Never mind the night before. They would deal with that, enjoy it, but later. Right now she knew what she had to do about Shalom.

That's just how she began their conversation: "I know what we have to do."

"Good morning, Ms Holland," he said, still clearly at least half asleep. "Is there something I can...?"

"You have to come," she said. "I need your computer and a better connection than I can get here. The hotel only has dial up, and it doesn't have enough speed. Do you have decent speed at your school? Marriage records. We have to look them up."

Marnie heard, and almost felt, Eli draw in a deep breath. "Of course," he said. "But, we eat breakfast first, right?"

Neither of them referred to the night before, even though Marnie had revisited the scene in the car, had repeated the words he'd said to her time and time again, and still felt his kiss. She had run her finger tips over her lips to capture his kiss forever.

But now there was something even more important, because it might free her forever.

Breakfast at the King David was the usual lavish Israeli buffet. A generous meal could be made from the Israeli specialties: hard-boiled eggs, salads, smoked fish, cheeses and amazingly rich yoghurt were only part of the offerings. With a breakfast like this you don't have to stop for lunch, Marnie thought. Except for what she already thought of as their special ritual; iced coffee in the late afternoon.

When the two of them got to Eli's *Yeshiva*, Marnie was surprised to find that there was a lot more going on than Eli had ever admitted. As *Rosh Yeshiva*, the head of the school, he even had a secretary to help him keep track of the student registrations coming in. There would be very real classes after the first of the year, he admitted.

"It was so quiet when I was here the first time," Marnie said, after she shook hands with his secretary.

"I only have her come half days, the regular work week, Sunday to Thursday, until noon. You just missed her the first time you were here. I was going for the sympathy vote at the time, so I sort of let you believe I needed students, teachers, everything."

"And lunch," Marnie said. "Don't forget you needed lunch."

"We both needed lunch," he agreed.

Marnie thumbed through all the letters piled on his desk.

"Canada, U.S.A, Australia, France. This is fabulous," she said. "And, I thought you were in BIG trouble?"

"Well, not so BIG," Eli admitted. "But I could still use an exceptional *Talmud* teacher; a teacher for a mixed class, or classes. They might not be the most advanced classes in the world, but they will be among the most egalitarian."

Did Eli have any idea how appealing the thought of such teaching would be to her? She didn't dare say that, or even think about it for too long. The thought of such a possibility, added to the kiss of the night before and the intimacy of their conversations so far, might melt her resolve away.

Did the kiss last night mean anything? After all, they were adults. It had been, it probably was, just an impulse of the moment. What would she give for it to mean more? Would meaning more, meaning everything, be worth a major shift in her career, in her whole life?

"I'm at the University of Judaism too, you know," she said, reminding herself, as much as telling Eli. "Turov is just a side thing," she said.

He nodded, as though he understood. "I know it's very hard to even think of giving up tenure at a major school." He looked unhappy.

Marnie noted the look on his face with a kind of wonder. Maybe last night . . . No, first the problem with Shalom. Eli had dropped the subject of her working in Israel, but it continued to resonate in her mind, even though it shouldn't.

Maybe she could take a six-month sabbatical and teach here. Would that allow her to see Liora and Sammy? No, this kind of day-dreaming was not a good idea.

Resolutely she went back to what had brought her to Eli's office; the research she had to do.

"I'm going to look up marriages in Israel,' Marnie said, sitting down behind Eli's desk when he indicated she should use his computer.

A few minutes later, she said. "Look, here it is. Here's my marriage to Shalom, and my *get*. And, his marriage to his next wife. Liora said her name was Esther. And, here's their *get*. It's all listed on a government data base."

It had not registered with Marnie, but Eli had moved away while she typed and was now standing next to his secretary at her desk just outside his office. He looked up when Marnie spoke. He could easily see her and hear her through the open door.

"Hang on, I'd like to see that," he said. But in the few moments it took him to cross the two small offices Marnie was suddenly struck by the shock of an idea galvanizing her. She began typing furiously.

As usual with Marnie, when she had a new idea, it was as though everyone around her, in this case Eli and his secretary, disappeared. With an especially compelling thought, all else vanished.

She had been asking herself the same question ever since Shalom had showed up: Why would he claim to need a divorce? Why would he torment her with such an idea? What would he gain from it?

But, what if he was right? What if he did need a divorce from her? Then she would need one too, from him.

A few minutes later Marnie sat back from the computer. She turned away from the machine, and all that she'd just learned from it. Somewhat to her surprise Eli was standing just a step away, behind her. She'd forgotten where she was.

"So, now we know," Eli said.

"You know too?" she said. How could this latest news, so unbelievable, be known by this man, known by anyone except her?

"I was reading over your shoulder," Eli said. "It didn't seem to bother you."

She hadn't been aware of him. At least he didn't look annoyed, the way some people did when an idea of hers blocked them out completely. Eli just smiled. When she stood up to get away from the hateful news on the computer he let her edge past him as she moved to the other side of his desk. Marnie sat down in one of the two visitors' chairs opposite the desk. Eli went back to his own desk chair.

Eli didn't have a very big office. There were only a few pieces of furniture. A black horozontal four-drawer file was positioned behind him, between the two windows. Both windows were covered on the outside with the ugly metal grille that was part of the new front that had been put on the building as a security measure, bomb-proofing.

Eli eased into his desk chair, one that would have dwarfed most men. Once seated, he spun around sideways and with one foot he reached for the upholstered leather camel saddle, red, blue and gilt, that he used as a footstool. It was standing in a corner, but he nudged it a few inches toward himself, until his long legs could reach it with ease.

Marnie clasped her hands together tightly, her head down. She might not have to pretend with Eli, since he'd seen what she had seen, but, now, even though it was clear, she couldn't imagine telling anyone else what she'd just found.

She perched on the edge of the chair. She dared not relax. If she did, something even more horrible might sneak up on her. No, that wasn't possible. There was nothing more horrible.

"I'm still married to him," she said, her voice very low. "I can't believe it."

"I believe it," Eli said. "It's all there in those American marriage records you called up. It's just as easy to find as the stuff in Israel."

"I'm still married to him in the States. I didn't just have a Jewish wedding; I had a civil wedding too." Marnie shuddered.

Eli got up and went to her. He knelt on the floor, to get to her eye level, to engage her. It seemed clear just for the moment he didn't feel he could touch her, couldn't hug her. It was also clear that hugging her was what Eli wanted to do. Why would anyone ever want to touch her again?

"Marnie, that's what most people do when they get married. The religious ceremony and the civil ceremony are together. Rabbis and cantors are licensed to do regular marriages. The religious ceremony is usually the add-on in most people's minds." Nothing Eli said made Marnie feel any better. She couldn't look him in the eye and her usual spirited response to a problem had vanished.

He tried again, speaking slowly, in a very matter-of-fact voice.

"You know the bride at a traditional Jewish service doesn't say anything. So it wouldn't have made a difference in the service. You and Shalom didn't know about it, that's all. And the guy who came from Israel to marry you, he probably didn't know either. If he signed the request to be able to perform a marriage, that's all that was needed. Rabbis who go to a different state to do weddings sign those documents all the time. My brothers and my father do it. I've done it a couple of times."

"Why? Why would anyone? Why would it have been done to us?" Marnie said, low, tentative. She was back to not knowing what question to ask. "Shalom wouldn't have done this. There was no advantage to him."

"I'd bet your parents did it to give you a bargaining chip," Eli said. "At a guess, that's what it has to be. I just don't know why they didn't tell you before," he said.

"My parents? Not my mother. This is my father's doing. I don't think I'll ever...."

Eli smiled and said, "You won't believe that he actually tried to do something for you? So you could eventually get back at Shalom?"

He was still kneeling so they would have been at direct eye level, except that Marnie kept looking down. He must have needed to look into her eyes very badly, because very gently, with one finger, he lifted her chin until they were finally looking at each other. His face was only inches from hers and apparently he could tell at the moment even that felt like an intrusion, so, he sighed, then, very gently he took that one finger away and rocked back on the balls of his feet to create a little extra space for her. But, he held her gaze, and she didn't feel it necessary to look down again.

"I don't know why your father didn't tell you, unless he was keeping it for a moment when it was needed. Maybe he knows this might be the moment. You want to do something for Liora. You want to stop Shalom from playing his marriage games. You can call your Dad and ask him why, you know," Eli said.

Marnie looked straight at him. He was smiling; trying to show her there was good in what was happening. She couldn't respond. Her face was frozen, jaw and mouth set like rock. "I didn't intend my marriage to be a political statement." She could barely speak. "Why wouldn't he have told me years ago?"

"Shalom never bothered you before, right? That's probably why. And you didn't want to get married again, so it didn't matter. You told me that. You said you'd never get married under this system. A civil American marriage might solve the problem, but you didn't pursue one. And you wouldn't marry someone who is not Jewish. So, he must have been keeping it for some time when it would be important."

"He can't make choices like that for me," Marnie said, the numbness she'd been feeling now being replaced with hostility.

"I can see you feeling that way, but I don't think he had that in mind. Maybe he didn't think it would take so long for you or Shalom to twig to it."

"What?" Marnie didn't even understand the point Eli was trying to make, she was so caught up in the horror of knowing that she was still married to Shalom and that her father had done this to her.

"Marnie, Shalom has been married one more time at least, but it was here in Israel. So, they never checked for an American divorce. He may be a bigamist in civil terms, but in Jewish, Israeli, terms, he's totally kosher."

"The system is outrageous," Marnie said, in a heated tone of voice.

"Yes, of course it's outrageous. I tried to use the system too, and look what happened to me." Eli might not be as angry as Marnie, but he obviously felt just as wronged. "Don't you see; we were both caught in the same trap; the stuff Shalom's been doing, selling his kid into 'near' marriages. And, whatever Sammy is doing, I'd bet it's part of the same thing, all part of the same system.

"It was one thing to keep men in line over a *get* when the local rabbi could threaten to excommunicate him if he didn't give his wife a *get,* or his union could say they wouldn't let him work. That stuff actually happened, and it worked. But how do you enforce it when people leave the country? And they're making it worse if they'll send a rabbi to the U.S. to marry someone in a Jewish-only ceremony. Your dad fought back. He actually did a good job. He did it to protect you. You were a kid. He's probably surprised it's taken so long to be put into play."

Eli must sound like this when he's teaching Marnie thought, irrelevantly. He's so logical, so coherent. I bet he's a wonderful teacher.

"I mean it's so dumb," Eli said, winding up his mini-lecture. "There was Shalom, with the best girl ever, and he's mean, he hits, he makes you leave. I don't understand him at all."

"But, if it's true, if I'd known, I," she clenched her fists.

"I'm going to kill him. That what I'm going to do, I'm going to kill him," Marnie said, as though she and Eli were having two totally different conversations.

Eli skittered back a few more inches, but stayed crouched on the floor and kept holding Marnie's gaze.

"You're going to kill Shalom? I know how you feel, but in this case I don't know that he had any more idea than you. Wouldn't a divorce be less violent?"

"No, I'm going to kill my father. Right after I phone him and thank him for trying to save me, I'm going to kill him. I just don't understand why he didn't tell me."

Eli stood up. "He knows you," he said. "He figured you'd do something noble, like grant Shalom the American divorce too."

Wanting to take the pressure off her, as much as possible, he said, "Anyway, you can think about it for a while. You're not going to call your Dad right now. It's the middle of the night in California."

"It's the middle of the night in California?" Marnie said. That seemed to cheer her up immensely.

Eli checked his wrist watch. "Well, roughly noon here. So, six a.m. in New York. Not too bad. That's three a.m. in California. About as middle of the night as possible. Why don't we just wait...?"

"Never mind killing him," Marnie said, and she pulled the cell phone she was using in Israel out of her bag.

"Watch me wake him up in the middle of the night. That will be worse than death to him."

✡

Walter rolled over in bed and picked up the phone. It might be three a.m., but he'd been waiting for this call ever since Marnie left for Israel. Normally he hated being awakened like this, but he was determined that he would wouldn't even sound groggy.

"Yes, hello," He said. He went on, his voice especially lively, "Marnie?"

"How do you know it's me, Daddy?" she demanded.

"Who else would call at this hour?" Her father said reasonably enough. "I assume everything is okay?"

146

"Dad," Marnie said, trying to sound stern. "What did you do to Shalom, and to me, when we got married?"

"Me?" Walter said, even managing to sound innocent, despite the time of the day. Amazing he could pull it off.

"I helped you get married as I recall. It was a big mistake, of course, but how were we to know?"

"Apparently you thought you knew better than us. What did you do?"

"Why? Have you met someone else you want to marry?" Walter said brightly.

"What has that got to do with anything?" she said, "And, what business is it of yours? I'm a grown up, you know."

She had dodged his question about meeting someone. That was a really good sign. He couldn't remember her ever doing that before. When he asked before, she'd always said, 'no,' very succinctly.

"Of course you're a grown up, honey. But you weren't when you married Shalom, so I built in a little insurance. That's all. Now it's paying off big time. You should have seen him when he was here. He still hadn't figured it out. I knew you would."

Beside him in their California king size bed – as big as the whole of Santa Barbara County – Walter always said, Beatrice opened her eyes and snapped on her bed-side lamp.

He mouthed the words: *Marnie knows*. You never had to explain things to Beatrice. She was almost as smart as their daughter, but much more practical.

Marnie's voice buzzed in his ears, "Dad, I thought I had a Jewish wedding only. That the *get* was all I needed. I know it cost a lot and I'm sorry, but whatever you did, or thought you did, it might be legal, but it's not ethical. Whatever you did or Shalom thinks you did it can't..."

"Oh yes it can," Walter said. "'Revenge, a dish best eaten cold,' was what some other genius once said. Well, we've had a dozen years for things to cool off."

"Dad." This was his daughter very close to tears. Walter felt terrible. But, he wasn't one bit sorry he'd done the deed. It was too bad Marnie had to suffer, even if it was only for a short time.

"Look sweetheart, Shalom brought 'his' rabbi from Israel to marry the two of you. That wasn't just sentiment you know. He understood what he was doing. Thanks to Dr. Schlumberger, I knew what he was doing too. With a Jewish marriage all he'd ever need was a *get*. Ball in his court. Well, I just made sure this rabbi-buddy of Shalom's was also a duly appointed official of the State of California. He was supposed to do that anyway, to perform a wedding legally. Ball in my court. Or, your court, if you prefer."

"Dad," Marnie started to speak again, but then she stopped, unable to go on. He took advantage of the silence. Marnie already understood this was no casual scheme on his part; but a well-thought-out plan that had just come to fruition.

"I just gave him the form within a flock of papers to sign – most of them about his free first-class trip to and from Israel, him and his wife, with them also getting all the travel points. He signed it. So when you got divorced you needed an American divorce too. It's not a big deal, but Shalom didn't know, and still doesn't. Although, he may also have figured it out by now. He will figure it out eventually."

"How did you figure it out?" he wanted to know. Walter sat up, plumping the pillows behind him. He wanted to hear this. What would she say?

"I had help," Marnie said.

She's met a guy, Walter thought, but he didn't say it.

"Dad. Dad." Marnie tried again, but she couldn't go on. Walter couldn't believe it. He'd rendered Marnie pretty well speechless.

"He's trying to marry an American. Her family was smart enough to do a search. They found Shalom Gasith is still married to Marnie Holland. I couldn't do a search all those years ago. It wouldn't have helped us anyway. But, yes, I did get those papers signed. And I'd do it again."

"But then I'm still married to him," Marnie said. He could hear the revulsion in her voice, the shock.

"Well, yes, you are. I'm sorry about that part. But, maybe there's something you want from him. You want a divorce. Our lawyer will have it done in minutes. Un-contested. You haven't lived together for more than a decade. There are no money issues, no issues over children. Unless you want there to be issues. There will be nothing to it. I've kept the lawyer up to date. Set it all up years ago.

"Do you want the lawyer's name right now? You can call him. Although maybe you want to wait an hour or two at least. Maybe you'd like to take Shalom's house in Israel or something. I don't know that you'd need it, but you sure could make him uncomfortable. It might even cost him money. Just remember, a divorce frees him to marry again. You too, of course. Not that you've ever wanted to marry anyone else."

He wanted to add, 'who isn't a *shmuck*,' but he didn't want to push things too far. "Maybe you've met someone, for example. Maybe you want things to move especially quickly for some reason." He finished somewhat anti-climactically.

All Walter got was silence. He'd managed to surprise her, to upset her. He could live with that. She'd figured it out herself, no surprise. He'd seen that brain of hers in action before. She just kept thinking about it, collecting a fact here, and a thought there, and then BINGO, one day she just knew.

He wasn't going to apologize for catching out Shalom Gasith. As soon as this day really got started, it would be a great one. He and Bea grinned at each other as he held onto the phone, waiting for Marnie to think of what to say next.

CHAPTER FOURTEEN

Sitting, relaxed, his feet up on his camel saddle foot-stool, Eli watched Marnie staring at the phone in her hand as though it was a living thing that might bite her.

"You'll never believe," she started to say as she clicked off the phone.

Eli had been aware of each and every one of her reactions while she spoke to her father. First of all, surprise, then a look of real revulsion, followed by the slim edge of the thought – she disliked the truth, but some good might come of what was going on. And, finally, though angry with her father, she was not going to kill him.

Despite Marnie's discomfort, which he hoped would soon pass, Eli was a happy man. He leaned back even further. Marnie would look to him for help with her situation. He knew it. He planned to be so ever-present she would take it as given he was part of the solution to all her problems. He wasn't going to say it; he would just do it. He already knew Marnie felt something more than friendship for him. He did not want simple friendship. Nor did he care they had just met. This was bigger, far bigger, than both of them. They'd both been waiting a long time for this. As he thought through what they had to do next his fingers tapped out a tune on the arm of his chair.

He wasn't certain exactly how he would proceed, but he was so acutely aware of her moods and thoughts he only needed to watch her closely. He'd been doing so since he met her.

Right now, Marnie was feeling vulnerable. So this would be the perfect time for both of them to be open to new ideas, new love, real love.

She was still trying to understand what the knowledge she had just gained meant and how to handle all the ramifications. Her confusion would not last long.

"You'll never believe what my father did. I don't know what to do. What does it all mean? He lied to me. Well, maybe not an outright lie, but he didn't tell me the truth," Marnie said.

"He fooled me…and Shalom….I'm still married to him, to Shalom; in the U.S. Can you believe it? .It makes my skin crawl. It makes we want to cry. It means…"

"It means you're in charge." Eli offered gently. He stood up, started toward her, but not too quickly. He didn't want Marnie to feel more pressure right now.

"What do you mean, I'm in charge?"

"Shalom needs that divorce. You want to talk to the kids. You negotiate. That's how people do it in the regular world. You talk to Liora when you want to. You take her shopping. Hell, legally she is still a kid, at least in America, where all this is going to happen. You could get visitation rights. You can try to reach out to Sammy. Maybe it's not too late to get to know Sammy."

"But, if Shalom doesn't want me to. It would be so… unethical… I mean…."

"Look, I know you don't normally think this way, but it must appeal to you on some level. That man made your life miserable. He made sure you loved his children and then he separated you from them. He didn't want you, a genius, to learn, especially Hebrew texts. He's a miserable, dishonest specimen, a lowlife. And what I'm saying is not *loshen hora*. There is no evil speech in this kind of talk when it's the truth; and I'm not saying it in public, just to you."

"So, he deserves to be punched out, have his eye blackened in his own front courtyard," Marnie suggested.

"Well, I'm not especially proud of that, but yes, he deserved it, and if I could get away with it, I might very well do it again."

"Eli, you don't mean you want to be violent?"

"He used violence on you, Marnie. And on others, I'm sure. And, he'll likely do it again. He certainly deserved to be paid back for what he's done before. Anyway, you don't have to do him any violence. Your dad has a hot-shot lawyer, I'm sure. Later today, when they are awake, your dad and the lawyer, really awake, we'll call and plan what to do next."

Eli was walking back and forth in the tiny space behind his desk chair, smacking one fist into the palm of his other hand. He stopped. He hadn't realized how much he really would like to hurt Shalom again. Since his Rattler days smacking anyone had been anathema to him.

"If you want to speed this up, for example, you could let Shalom know what happened. You could even tell him you're doing it because it's the ethical thing to do. And, at the same time, you can tell him you want this or that, whatever you decide.

"Or, you might let your father tell him all about it. I bet your dad would love to do the job."

He could see her relaxing a little as he spoke. He had just delivered what had been a long speech for him, but he wanted her to have some time. The news she could be free in new ways, was beginning to creep into her brain, coming right after the news that she had been bound and not really known it. Marnie was so smart. But, when it came to people she was either naïve, way too honorable, or unaware of how most peoples' minds worked.

"Israel would no longer be off limits to me, even when Shalom is here," Marnie said, in a kind of wondering voice.

She got right to the heart of the issue. If they were to be a couple, the most important thing to Eli, she had to able to travel between homes in America and Israel, without fear.

Her brain, and hopefully her heart, had taken her to the most important place. She didn't have to avoid Israel any longer. She could have Israel, and him, in her life. Eli knew she hadn't made all those connections yet. But she would. He would make sure of it.

For once he was the one thinking faster. He'd already built a fantasy life around being with her. Last night he'd moved one small step toward making it real; an embrace, one real kiss. Maybe it wasn't such a fantasy?

He shouldn't get ahead of himself, not go there yet, but he couldn't help it: *It's my fantasy, I suppose I can go wherever I choose.*

Consider, if our kids are just like her, I'll have Marnie as a model in front of me all the time, and her parents to talk to, so I'll know what to do. If we have kids like me, the Lord will have to help us.

He really was way ahead of himself, already considering a family, and the options of a career for Marnie with part of the year in each country, Israel and the U.S.A.

Since he'd spent so much time at her conference, he now had a real sense of Marnie's academic standing. She already had an amazing reputation. Tenure in Talmud at her age was almost unheard of. She should be, would be, internationally known. He would make sure of it, if that was what she wanted.

He would make sure she was loved. Make sure she was never afraid again.

He couldn't just stand there, leaving any barrier between them. Barriers were being swept away, one after another. He didn't want to frighten her; but, he couldn't just let things stay as they were. Circumstances needed a push and he was the man to do it.

"Your father actually out-smarted you," he said, allowing himself to smile at the thought. The situation was not without humor. "How often does that happen? He must be enjoying himself. Maybe his enjoyment is just a little too much for your comfort? Give him some time. He's waited a long time for this. Think of what went into raising you."

She'd told him about learning French and Italian on a month-long trip to Europe when she was four, entering college at fourteen, working on her PhD at eighteen. He didn't envy her parents, raising such a child.

He was going to live with Marnie as the center of his life. He wasn't quite sure how it would come about, but he was certain about it. He knew Marnie had feelings for him. He could assure himself on that point at least. Even if no one else knew yet, he knew it. Their love would be the basis of the rest of their lives.

When they were living in California, if they had to live in California part time, one of his brothers, or his assistant, would take over at the Yeshiva. Never mind he didn't have an assistant yet, or anything he really needed assistance with. Nor did he have any idea if one of his brothers might want the job.

He could see how genuinely uncomfortable Marnie was with what had to happen in the next few days. She'd put away her phone, but was sitting far forward, perched on the edge of her chair, not touching the back. Her arms were folded in her lap, as though trying to make herself as small a target as possible. But she'd maintained eye contact with him.

"We'll have to think what this means to us," she said. She flushed. "What it means to me." Her correction was her only acknowledgment of what she'd said the first time.

"No. For us. You were right the first time." Eli said. In two strides he was around the desk. He took her hand, pulled her upright; put his arms around her, pushing the door to his office shut at the same time. He could feel a tremor through Marnie's whole body; her reaction to his embrace. He pulled her closer.

"Do you remember what I said last night," he said. Their faces were only inches apart. Who would have thought he'd find a woman like this; brilliant, beautiful, even just the right height?

"Last night?" Marnie said. It was a question, not an answer.

"Do you remember? In the car?" He kissed her once, gently, just as he finally had last night, watched as a flush bloomed on her neck and cheeks. She was so beautiful, and so responsive. Responsive to him. They would need to find a way to manage this; a way to fully fall in love, to express that love, not in some way designed for shy children. The old rules wouldn't work for them. They would have to work out a unique system for their unique situation.

Marnie said. "You said, you said." She kissed him this time. "There. That was part of what you said. I didn't forget."

"No, you didn't forget," he agreed happily.

Their arms around each other tightened. Her arms were around his neck. But, he felt her anxiety, felt her clutch at the back of his shirt. "But, I'm still married, Eli. I can't believe it, but I'm still married."

"Doesn't matter," he said. "We'll wait. Both of us want to do this the right way. Now we know what the problem is, and how to fix it, we can wait. For the first time in years you know exactly where you stand. We know Shalom isn't going to give you any trouble. He isn't going to give me any trouble either. But, we won't give him anything to fight back with either, so we have to behave. Just remember everything we've done and talked about. Everything."

He kissed her again, passionately enough to imprint how he felt about her. Then he loosened his grip. "You have to sit down," he said, gently guiding her back to her chair. He took a step back. "My secretary is a nice *frum* lady. She'll be suspicious if this goes on too long. But, the same as last night, right? We both need to remember; to know where we are. Not to have to start over again and again. We don't have time for starting over again and again. We'll need to sort all this out once and for all."

"I'll remember," Marnie assured him. Then she sat back in her chair, managing to look serious and somewhat aloof. Who would guess Marnie was also a good actor?

Inside, Eli felt, almost heard, a click. He doubted that Marnie realized – he was just figuring it out himself – part of him enjoyed all of this; even the confusion of her still being married, even the limitations on how to behave. All that was Rattler. The part of him he'd long ago tried first to control and then to blot out. It had been his music and his imagination, but also the most dangerous part of him.

He'd thought he might have to work without those things for the rest of his life. But suddenly, with this woman, Rabbi Marnie Holland, for the first time, he knew he could have Rattler back in his life.

Doors were opening for Marnie, no matter how cautious she might feel. Eli was experiencing the same thing, but he was further ahead on what it meant. Whole vistas were opening to him. He could project his life and Marnie's into a future for both of them.

Two disparate parts of Eli's being had just coalesced. Suddenly he had permission to be whole. He hoped she would soon feel the same. She'd been fighting the battle brought about by those years when she'd been married to Shalom and all the years after, when she had not allow herself to love. Probably she'd never thought of it in that way, just as he hadn't consciously known SerpentSity's Rattler was still there, right under his skin.

He welcomed Rattler back, the adventurous, daring, creative side of him. Now he didn't need the hell raiser, the young man who hadn't known what to do with the requirements his family had put upon him, the expectations. He could welcome the parts of Rattler he'd like to keep. Marnie would understand; as soon as he figured out how to tell her.

CHAPTER FIFTEEN

When she woke the next morning, Marnie did not know what to do with herself. After the disclosures of the day before, the talk with her father, a discussion with the lawyer in Santa Barbara, after Eli making himself clear on how he felt about her, she should feel wonderful. But she didn't. Probably too much had happened.

Their beautiful hotel room looked dreary. The only sound was Tovah showering. Marnie glanced at the phone. The message light was definitely not on. Who would have left a message? You talked to your parents. Eli brought you back to the hotel so late. They had sat in his car for what seemed like hours, making out like teenagers.

What's wrong? But, she didn't even respond to her own question. She just lay there. Did she have to get out of bed?

There didn't seem to be a good reason to get up today. She didn't have a date with Eli, not so far anyway, not for breakfast, lunch or dinner. They weren't going to visit Liora again until Wednesday evening at the earliest, and this was only Tuesday. The news she was still married to Shalom was the single most depressing piece of news she'd ever experienced. Even if it could be fixed quickly it wasn't going to get fixed today. No matter how fast her father worked, she was still married to that man. Plus, she couldn't really rush. She needed to make use of the situation, for the sake of the children, if not herself. She had to. That depressed her as much as the situation itself. How had she come to be required to negotiate, to outsmart Shalom?

Her father had promised to work with their lawyer in Santa Barbara, making sure to see about finally and totally ending whatever idiotic relationship she had with Shalom. Her Dad had also promised that if Shalom called, he would get a phone number where Marnie could reach him. It occurred to her that she could also leave a message for Shalom by emailing the staff list at the Turov *Yeshiva*. She framed the message in her mind, as she would have liked to send it. If she dared, it would have read like this:

"Would the backbiting lowlife, who thinks women don't count for anything, please inform Shalom Gasith – if you know him, you'll know how to reach him, and you know who you are. Ask him to supply a phone number where Rabbi Marnie Holland can reach him. Urgent!!

I'll send it myself, she conceded. She knew it would be a perfectly respectful note. But, just to make a point, rather than going through the official school email system, where they would edit out the word 'Rabbi" wherever it appeared, before they sent it on, I'll go around them, and I'll sign "Rabbi," too. Maybe they'd tell me not to come back. Hmmmm?

Then she could stay…no, she wasn't going there, not even in her most vivid imaginings.

Well, she would get up, she decided. She would send the email to the *Yeshiva* as soon as she was fully awake and could get to the computer center in the hotel. She would even edit what she wanted to say into a masterpiece of restraint. At the moment, though, she could only consider what she'd really like to say, and what she would say to Shalom eventually.

To her way of thinking it was unethical, even shameful, to insist on certain things before she offered Shalom the divorce. There was no question about what had to be a part of the deal. She had to be able to see Liora regularly and Sammy too, if he wanted to meet with her, either in Israel or in California. If she wanted to arrange for the children to travel, it had to be allowed. She had to take part in discussions of whether Liora would go to school, work or marry. She had to have the opportunity to talk with her step-son, Sammy. She even wanted to talk to the women who had been stepmothers to the children, if possible, and see what they could add to what she already knew about the children.

As she was thinking this through, she wondered if she should tell Liora to ask her father for his phone number. What better way to get Shalom's attention? Would it be good or too damaging for Liora to have a part in all this?

The phone rang. She didn't want to hope it was Eli – he had to work sometime – but her voice was extremely pleasant as she picked it up. "Yes, Rabbi Holland, here."

It was the front desk of the Hotel. It seemed there was a young woman looking for her.

Within a second Liora was on the house phone, babbling in rapid Hebrew. She was in trouble. Sammy was in trouble. She didn't know how to reach *Abba*. Sammy always did that. And she knew she'd promised she'd not tell *Abba*...

"Sh, Sh, Liora, it'll be okay. You can tell your *Abba* everything now. But, stop for a minute. How did you know I was here?" Marnie asked. She hadn't told Liora which hotel, as a way of slowing down Shalom if he learned she was in Israel.

"You said you were at a conference," Liora said. "I started with the top hotels, The King David, The Hilton. I tried the King David first."

Obviously there was nothing wrong with Liora's ability to think a problem through.

Behind Marnie, Tovah came out of the bathroom wrapped in one of the hotel's thick white terrycloth robes.

"Eli?" she mouthed, smiling hugely.

"No," Marnie said. She spoke into the phone again. "Liora, wait just one minute." Then, covering the receiver for a moment, she looked Tovah straight in the eye, willing her to listen, and not comment. Not yet, anyway.

"It's my stepdaughter. At least a long time ago she was my stepdaughter. There's a big problem with her brother and my ex-husband, who is an Israeli. I'd like to have her come up here. Are you okay with that?"

Tovah sat down on her bed, hard. She nodded, barely, stunned. Tovah was about to find out answers to all the questions she'd ever had about Marnie, and more than she'd ever guessed. If Marnie felt any victory in holding on to the news for so long, was it a defeat because Tovah now knew? It didn't feel like a defeat. It felt liberating. One thing for sure, there were going to be a lot of questions to answer later on.

Marnie knew perfectly well Tovah wouldn't care who she invited to their room, but asking her permissions was as good a way of passing on her startling news as Marnie could think of.

Tovah didn't ask a single question. In fact she didn't say a word. She just stayed where she was, sitting on the side of her bed for much longer than Marnie might have expected.

Why would she ask questions? Tovah was very quick. She'd realize that in minutes she would know everything about Marnie's past. Since this was Tovah, she'd remember everything too; every detail that had been missing for all the years she and Marnie had known each other.

✡

It was hours later when Marnie wished she had been able to see Tovah's face when Liora came to the door and fell into her arms, wailing, "*Ima Malka*, what am I going to do? What am I going to tell *Abba* about Sammy?" It seemed to Marnie that Eli arrived almost at the same moment.

Liora looked horrified for a moment or two, then she said to Marnie, "If he is your friend, and I am not alone with 'him,' it is okay. Sammy is more important than 'him.'"

"He is my friend," Marnie said. Eli smiled at Liora, trying to break the ice, but the girl looked right through him. One day, Marnie thought, she'll call him by name and it will be alright. If she married Eli? No, she wasn't going there. What impact would that have on Liora?

Tovah had ordered breakfast for all of them and had been on the phone. She must have been the one to ask Eli to come over. It was as though the kind of family problems Marnie had missed from the time she had left Sammy and Liora as small children had suddenly caught up with her, creating a vortex of people, talk, food and activity in one large room at the King David Hotel.

Dimly she'd heard Tovah make several other phone calls, asking various people at the conference to take over some of her duties. Tovah wasn't going anywhere, and Marnie was grateful her friend willingly answered the phone, offered food and drink to Liora, briefed Eli. Wait until Tovah found out that Eli knew the whole story of her past before she did. She would not like that one bit.

As it developed, Liora story was this: she had come home from seeing Marnie and found Sammy on the phone with their father. They were shouting at each other. At least Sammy was shouting and Liora assumed her father was doing the same.

"I bet it's not her family. I bet she doesn't want to marry you," Sammy hollered into the phone. "Not because of some law there. You're an old man. That's why."

"He said that to *Abba*," Liora said, clearly horrified. Her eyes were huge. She'd never heard her brother say anything like that to their father. Liora was going on and on in rapid fire Hebrew. It was fortunate everyone, Marnie, Tovah and Eli spoke Hebrew, so there was no need to translate, or slow Liora down.

This morning when she got up, Liora said, Sammy was gone. Luggage was gone too, and all his clothes. And *Abba's* little truck. She'd left Sammy a note, telling him where she could be found. She'd also left a message on his cell phone, telling him where she would be this morning.

Eli nodded. "Adolescence often hits in the *frum* community later than in other places. Because of early marriages and things, it doesn't play out the same way as it does in the States. Believe me, I know. Sammy is overwhelmed. He's afraid he'll be getting married. He's afraid he won't be getting married. He envies his father, and he's repulsed at the same time. I don't know how his work factors into this. Is he in competition with his father?"

For the first time Liora spoke directly to Eli, "*Abba* doesn't want Sammy doing things he doesn't understand. But Sammy does it anyway. And, Sammy said that when *Abba* gets home, with Katie or without, married or not, he'd be gone. He meant it. He was already gone this morning."

"Where would he go?" Marnie said.

Liora wailed, long and loud. 'I don't know. Where would he go? He has friends, but he wouldn't go to them. He'd never admit he needed to leave home."

The phone rang again, and as she had all morning, Tovah picked it up. She listened, asking, in Hebrew, 'Who is this please? Who do you want to speak to?"

Tovah held the phone up to Marnie. "It's Sammy. He wants to know if you are holding his sister a prisoner here to get back at their father?"

The word 'prisoner' went off like a bomb in the room, but instead of adding to the general din, it silenced everything.

Eli stopped eating. Marnie, her arm around Liora – they were sitting together on a small sofa in the TV area of the room – froze in place. Liora stood up. Her face was suddenly pink. "What does he mean, I'm a prisoner?"

Liora got up and took the portable phone out of Tovah's hand. She turned away, crossed the room. She spoke urgently, but quietly. No one could tell what she was saying.

This is like watching a silent movie, Marnie thought.

Eli went to the breakfast table room service had wheeled in. He poured a cup of coffee, adding cream and sugar. He sat down beside Marnie in the spot Liora had just vacated. "Here," he said. "Sorry, there's no ice cream, the way we usually like it."

He gestured toward the girl who stood, her back to them, holding the phone to one ear and gesticulating, as though her brother could see her.

"See," Eli said. "She's giving him hell. I have sisters, but it didn't save me from doing stupid stuff at that age. I think it was actually required. My sisters were always giving me hell."

"Required," Marnie said. "What's required? Not everybody does stupid stuff." Marnie was clutching the coffee that Eli had handed her. He'd brought it to her especially. It was wonderful coffee, even without ice cream.

"I doubt he's going to start a rock group, or trash a hotel room," Marnie whispered to Eli. They were all trying to hear what Liora was saying to her brother, but they could not. Liora remained turned away from the room.

Eli, Marnie and Tovah were grouped together now, giving the girl as much privacy as possible.

"You've certainly made this trip something special," Tovah said to Marnie. "And to think, you didn't want to come to this conference."

Marnie was watching Liora hunched over the phone, listening, then arguing. "Maybe I shouldn't have. I've caused so much trouble."

"You should have," Eli said with undeniable certainty.

"Just how long were you going to carry this thing around with you? Another decade or two?" Tovah asked. "If I'd known about it, it would have been settled when we were here for our first year. If I had known..."

"Tovah, it wasn't for you to solve it. It was my problem."

Tovah just snorted. It might not have been ladylike. It certainly wasn't very rabbinic; but it was expressive.

Tovah was a problem solver. "This should have been finished a long time ago," she insisted.

From where he sat beside Marnie, Eli said, "I think her timing is perfect."

CHAPTER SIXTEEN

iora spent the twenty minutes after speaking to her brother staring out one of the windows of Marnie and Tovah's room.

"Watching for Sammy," Eli said. "His coming here won't do us any good, you know. Even if she gave him hell on the phone, she'll go with him if he insists. Or, he'll threaten to tell their father. You both know that, right?"

"I'm not so sure she'll go," Marnie said, although she couldn't have given a very strong logical reason for her feelings about Liora, except surprisingly, there seemed to be a strong link between the two of them. The girl had come to her.

"My God," Tovah said. "She's not much older than Ari, and he's a California kid, and not *frum*. In fact Ari's probably a lot more sophisticated, more worldly. Marnie, you can't just let her go."

Marnie was still sitting on the small sofa, Eli close beside her. His long arm lay on the back of the sofa. He wasn't touching Marnie, but their posture felt intimate. She felt protected.

Eli leaned forward. His arm touched Marnie's back and shoulders. She shivered slightly; Eli would feel her body responding to his touch. That was quite wonderful. And wonderful, too, she didn't feel as though she had to pull away. Eli got up, found a sweater and draped it over Marnie's shoulders. It was a casual gesture, but profound, meaningful. Tovah's eyes went round. Marnie just smiled at her, her look telegraphing, 'more later.'

Eli sat down beside her again. "I'm more impressed with her now than when I thought I might marry her. I couldn't really hear, but she wasn't taking any crap. Maybe you're right. Maybe she'll stick around no matter what Sammy wants, or threatens," Eli said.

Tovah had taken a seat on a bench they'd pulled up to the breakfast table. She almost fell over backward. "You were going to marry her?"

"Well, no, not in the end. But her father, Marnie's ex, runs this *shatchan* business. Most of it is one scam after another. I thought I'd get married that way, totally *kosher*, you know."

Tovah was not very impressed. "You're hardly a kid, Eli, she said. "And not orthodox. But you felt you needed a *shatchan*. Why?"

"Kind of a checkered past," Eli said, briefly.

"It seemed like a good idea to him," Marnie said crisply.

"At the time," Eli said. "Only at the time; and not for very long."

Tovah's look at Marnie, confirmed what her first glance had said: Okay, I want the details on this one. Eli was going to marry this child?

Marnie didn't say a word. She just nodded ever so slightly; confirmation Tovah would know all the details once they had a chance to speak privately. It did seem the whole truth, her whole truth, was much easier to deal with than keeping up the road blocks and the 'no entrance' signs. All the barriers she'd felt she'd needed until – until Israel? Until she couldn't keep everything a secret anymore? Until Eli came into her life?

She didn't try to answer those questions. She just let them roll around in her brain for the moment. The answers would come.

Liora, still standing at the window, made a small noise. Marnie got up and crossed over to the girl, putting one hand on her shoulder. Liora leaned back against her slightly, which worried Marnie. Was this child so hungry for protection, for love? No wonder an early marriage seemed like such a good idea.

But Liora seemed to have moved back, mostly so she could point out the window at a very small van pulling into a parking space. The small truck had to be almost as old as Liora. Its paint had lost any gloss it once had. The top and body where faded to a dull light grey, probably the bare metal. Both doors had been replaced. They were different from the body; one red and one dark blue.

"That's *Abba's* car," Liora said. "Sammy says that before Abba comes home, he's going to buy a car."

"Does he have money for a car?" Marnie asked, wondering if helping Sammy with that kind of a purchase would help or hurt her case with her one-time stepson. Cars for youngsters were not common in Israel. Nothing like they were in California.

Liora edged closer and closer to the window watching Sammy's foreshortened figure until he disappeared under a roof ledge leading to the hotel's entrance off the parking lot.

Within two minutes there was a knock on the door.

"I'll get it," Eli said and both Marnie and Tovah, even Liora, obviously concurred. A protective male presence seemed like a very good idea.

CHAPTER SEVENTEEN

arnie had only seen Sammy one time, walking with Liora and then running for the bus as she and Eli had watched. Her impression had been accurate. Sammy looked 'hip,' almost fashionable. His garb may have been traditional, but his hat was the highest quality felt, his belt and suspenders were tooled black leather, items her father might have worn. His short black boots had a high gloss. He was armed with a pager and a PDA, both clipped to the waist of his black trousers. A computer case swung from one shoulder.

Without acknowledging anyone else in the room, he spoke to his sister in Hebrew, "Why are you here? You need to leave. You must come with me."

"We all speak Hebrew, Sammy." Eli said. He moved closer to the younger man. Eli's height intimidated Sammy somewhat. She hoped the affluence of the hotel itself and their large room, the lavish breakfast set out, all let the boy know that he was not in charge. Plus, Liora wasn't having any of what Sammy was saying, a pleasant surprise to Marnie.

"Why should I go with you? You said you were moving out. Your stuff is not at home anymore, so you have moved out. You've left me alone until *Abba* gets back. You told *Abba* that once he comes back, married or not, with Katie — Chava — or not, you would be gone. You said you would buy your own car. You don't need *Abba* anymore. You said so. So, why would you need me?"

"So, if not you, who will look after me?" Sammy said. He was trying for a light touch, but his less-than-perfect English, and his accent, destroyed the affect he was after. At least it did for Marnie. Sammy seemed more concerned about his impact on everyone else in the room, than about his sister. Probably he expected her to help him carry off the idea that she was his responsibility, his concern, and no worry of theirs.

Sammy turned and surveyed the group in front of him. Liora was standing behind him. Sammy would think he was there as a shield, but Marnie could see from Liora's face just how angry the girl felt.

"Ah, the *Rav*, who was all set to marry my sister," Sammy said dismissively, "A Conservative *Rav*, of course, so who cares?" It was clear he didn't take Eli seriously. "And, my one-time whore stepmother and her whore friend. It was to be; they are the same."

Whores. *Zonot*. There was a collective gasp from Eli, Marnie and Tovah. They were all on their feet now, moving toward Sammy.

Sammy had turned back to Liora, as though his comment should have convinced her to go with him. He reached out to her, not meaning to touch, but with a gesture that said, "See what they are? You must come with me."

Sammy was surprised when Liora backed away from him, her hands behind her back, as though to lessen even the possibility of contact.

Sammy was even more surprised when a hand, Eli's, clamped on his shoulder, spinning him around.

"Tell me you don't mean what you just said. Believe me; you've just made a big mistake. You want to reconsider, I'm sure. Let's say you spoke out in momentary anger and stupidity."

Marnie had to give Sammy some credit. He reacted quickly. He cocked his fist and said, with utter disdain. "I'm the Gasith who hits back. You tried to ruin my sister, you beat up my father, but you won't do either to me!"

But Eli wasn't planning to hit; Marnie could tell.

"I don't crush worms," Eli said. "But you will apologize to these women, and then you will sit down. You'll even apologize to me for your tone of voice.

"Believe me, you don't want to posture here and make like a big *macher*, when all you are is a worm. We won't believe anything you say, anyway, even the insults. But you will apologize!"

Eli's hand was still clamped on Sammy shoulder. He spun the younger man around, pushing him into a small armchair near the breakfast table.

"Now, apologize, or we will have nothing to do with you."

"I'll...I'll tell my father," Sammy blustered, sounding like a ten year old.

"Why would *Abba* help you now? *Abba* won't care what they do to you," Liora said. "*Abba* only cares about getting married. *Abba* might even stay in Indiana, with Katie. You can go there. You can end up in *Gehenna* for all I care."

Marnie doubted Liora had ever told her brother to go to Hell before, in English or Hebrew. Was it the girl's anger speaking or fear? Both?

Marnie moved to where Liora stood. She put her arm around the girl's shoulders. She could feel Liora's whole body vibrating.

"Marnie will look after me. Say you're sorry, Sammy, or there will be nothing to talk about. You don't believe for one minute they are *zonot*. And, in their world they are even both rabbis, even if not by us. You can't pretend they're not."

Liora recognizing something beyond her own world was a revolution, Marnie thought. I could make her understand, acknowledge some things. I need more time with her.

Sammy had the grace to look embarrassed, but his apology, a mumbled, "Sorry," spoken toward the floor, not looking at any of them, Eli, Tovah or Marnie, was grudging.

Then Sammy looked up. "What did you expect me to do? Just let you keep her here, in this kind of a place?" His glance around the elegant room suggested they were in some sort of slum.

Eli said crisply, "No one is keeping her here. She came on her own. She found Marnie on her own. And 'here' is a top-rated, totally kosher hotel. My father eats here. All the *Rabbonim* do. Apologize, Sammy." He walked so close to the chair he had pushed Sammy into, the younger man had to look straight up.

At six-foot-four plus, with the anger radiating off Eli's usually good-natured face, Sammy was right to be intimated.

"Okay, okay," Sammy said. This time he looked at both Marnie and Tovah. I'm sorry. You're not whores. But, you're not rabbis either!"

Tovah jumped in. "Well, I'm relieved to hear at least I'm not a whore. How in the hell would you know a whore if you saw one. And, if you do, what have you been doing?

"If my son even thought that word, I'd…" she stopped, unable to go on. Tovah had forgotten to speak Hebrew, so Marnie wasn't certain Sammy understood everything she said.

Marnie reached over, poured Sammy a cup of coffee, gestured to the table. "Eat something, Sammy. I accept your apology."

She was far from certain she'd ever really forgive this…this…twerp, but she doubted anyone could figure that out right now. Right now it didn't matter.

"I can see you are upset. But, how could you believe for one minute that I'd kidnap Liora. That I'd kidnap any-one? You've spent too much time listening to your father."

Sammy practically spit out the words. "My father is too busy with his… his fiancée to know what is going on."

He gave the word a twist that made it sounds as bad as the word 'whore.' "Do you expect me not to worry about my sister?"

Marnie sat down next to Tovah on the crowded bench. Liora stood behind the small couch where Eli had been sitting before. Marnie knew she wouldn't sit there for fear Eli would come and sit beside her.

"Tell them," the girl said. "You need me to run an office for you. You don't want to look after me, find me a *chatan*, a groom, they say in English. You want… you just need a helper for your business. One you don't have to pay, because if you move out of the store and the house, you'll have to pay rent. So your helper might as well be me. Never mind I already run the office for *Abba*. You want to take me away from *Abba*."

Liora's anger overwhelmed her and she turned around, crying.

Marnie got up to go to Liora. She took the girl in her arms and led her to the sofa, offering her a tissue and a glass of water. Liora grasped both as though they would save her.

Eli moved to an extra straight-back chair beside the desk and perched on it.

At the same time, the three of them: Eli, Tovah and Marnie all said, at the very same moment: "What business?"

CHAPTER EIGHTEEN

Along with Tovah and Marnie, Eli realized right away that asking Sammy about his business got them the boy's complete attention. His worries over his sister disappeared. He gathered up the breakfast dishes and wheeled the room service table out the door, obviously more comfortable, more familiar with the ins and outs of major hotels, than Eli thought he ought to be.

Not for the first time, Eli wondered at the Sammy's clothing and 'style.' The 'hip' quality the young man managed to project was very different from the usual Mea Shearim boy, who would not be sophisticated enough to be comfortable at the King David.

"Some of my clients stay here," Sammy said. "This is a nicer room than some, but you ought to see the suites. You should have rented one of them. Then you'd have lots of room."

Marnie was watching Sammy though narrowed eyes. "A suite at the King David?" she said.

"Sure," Sammy said. He closed the door on the breakfast table, turned, pulled the room's small desk away from the wall so he could plug in his lap top and connect to the hotel's web. He moved a couple of chairs so everyone could see the screen.

"You all think all I do is work with *Abba*. Well, I've got my own ideas!" he bragged.

Liora had turned pale. "Sammy, the *Rav* said you have to stop. What you are doing isn't...."

"Isn't kosher," Sammy said. "Who cares? The clients like it, and I can make a living. A good living. Especially if I don't have to work with *Abba*. It'll be a good enough living to look after you, so you won't have to stay with *Abba* and his latest. Sorry, Marnie. I know you were one of them"

"I've already forgiven you once, Sammy. Don't push it," Marnie said. Sammy's glib use of the word 'clients' clearly worried her.

Eli headed back to confront the boy – Sammy may have been a man to some people, his clients, but to Eli he was a boy, a brat.

Sammy stepped neatly behind the desk and bent down to check the plug and other connection of the computer. He flipped up the screen so Eli had trouble getting to him. Eli noticed that it was one of the newest laptops, with a very large screen.

"Sorry, *Rav*," Sammy said, "Why don't you just sit down and watch."

"I suppose I can slug you later," Eli muttered, not being in the least humorous. He went back to sit beside Marnie on the small sofa. Liora remained standing behind them, while Tovah perched on the end of her bed, not too far from Liora.

"Ladies and Gentleman," Sammy said, I bring you..."
His accent had almost totally evaporated. This was a
practiced presentation. Sammy had clicked through to
a website for www.yourIsraelConneXion.il.

Eli and the others watched as Sammy's 'pitch'
unfolded; pictures of the Wailing Wall, the remains of
Solomon's Temple, considered a holy place. Many in
Israel came to pray there regularly. The flood-lit plaza in
front of the Wall was alive with men in black suits and
hats and white shirts, most of them wrapped in prayer
shawls. The pictures that Sammy clicked through had
obviously been taken at a big holiday.

"I didn't advertise this at all. No expensive publicity
or advertising." Sammy said. "Startup costs was, were,
they were nothing, *gornisht*," he said, used the slang
Yiddish term for 'nothing' with relish.

"Not one red cent," the boy crowed. "I put flyers in
the hotels. The concierges in the up-scale hotels let me
do that, and I meet with people who are visiting."

That explained the Sammy's ease in the hotel room.

"My *Rav* doesn't like it," Sammy said easily, "But
he hasn't liked what *Abba* is doing for years, and that
doesn't stop my father. I offer a way for people to make
sure their memories of loved ones, saying *Kaddish in*
Israel, are carried out. Things like that."

Eli was impatient. "Lots of groups will say *Kaddish*
for you in Israel," Eli said. "People have asked me to say
Kaddish for someone at the wall. It's no big...."

"It's no big deal," Sammy interrupted smoothly, "But,
people don't trust the big groups, they trust a nice *frum*
kid much more."

This time Liora interrupted, "But they shouldn't.
He doesn't really do it. He says he will; he takes the

money. He makes it perpetual if the clients want it, but he doesn't do it. And, if you ask for a note in the wall, *a kvital,* he does the same thing. He makes a computer list and does them every few weeks, or even months. He doesn't find a *yeshiva bocher,* a student from a *yeshiva,* to say *Kaddish,* or write the notes.

"If someone asks you to write a note, you should do it. I think a real *sofer,* a real scribe, should write it."

"Why?" Sammy said, clearly wishing Liora would sit down and shut up.

"Why? I'm not breaking any religious rule. There's no *mitzvah* that says you have to leave a note in the wall. It's just a custom, a *minhag,* and it's like idolatry if you ask me. Like the wall is more holy then other places. You could leave a *kvital* at the Israel Museum, at the Museum of The Book, where the Dead Sea Scrolls are stored, why not? What difference would it make? You didn't mind when I bought you new things, or just made sure you had *sh'kelim,* money, in your pocket. *Abba* never gives you money, and he takes your paychecks from the *gan* where you work. He wants your money. I give you money!"

"But I don't take it anymore," Liora answer snapped back. "I don't take not even one *grosh* from you; not the smallest coin. Isn't that true? When I found out what you were doing, that the *Rav* doesn't like it, that it isn't honest! Since I know he doesn't approve, I haven't taken a penny."

Sammy had stepped back. Oddly, though he was angry at Liora's tirade, he also looked hurt. Like a little boy whose mother or father had just slapped the hand in the cookie jar.

Savagely Sammy pulled the electrical cord of the computer out of the wall and disconnected the internet.

"Fine," he said. "You don't approve. You don't want my money. That's just fine.

"*Abba* doesn't care about the *Rav* or he would have run his business better years ago. He wouldn't keep getting married either. You know Chava, Katie, is only the latest. A year, maybe two, and there will be another one. Eventually he'll give up on young girls and start on old women. That's what I would do, if I were *Abba*."

"Sammy." It was the only word Eli had heard from Marnie in all the time the boy had been talking. She looked horrified.

Eli knew Marnie felt as though she'd failed with Sammy, even if she hasn't seen him in a dozen years. Somehow she believed she should have had a lifelong impact. He put his hand or her arm, but Marnie stood up, so he wasn't certain she felt his gesture of support.

"Sammy," Marnie started again, but the boy interrupted her.

"It's your fault. Your *Abba* paid mine to divorce you and he realized, well, maybe he knew before, but with you it was a lot of money. At least with my mother, and Liora's, it was only the house, some furniture. Not so much money. He told us. So, marrying is like being a prostitute, a *zonah*, except a man can't be one, and anyway, it's legal for him to marry. But, not this time, for some reason. So, I'm improving on what *Abba* does, but I don't have to get married again and again. *Abba* can't do what I do. He doesn't understand computers and certainly not the Internet."

Sammy's English was slipping, Eli realized, losing that practiced edge. Cleverly he had hired someone, a professional, for his computer show, someone with one of those smooth British-inspired Israeli accents; someone who sounded as suave as Abba Eben, like a college professor.

"On the Internet, I'm a lovely *frum* kid who will do you a favor in the Holy Land. I'll make sure your 'loved one'..." Sammy's face when he used the term 'loved one' was murderous. "So, your hero, your family members, will forever be remembered in Israel. A few hundred dollars, or a few thousand, and it will be perpet...perpetu..." The word stopped Sammy momentarily.

"It will be eternal, until the Messiah comes. It's good enough for strangers who don't know me, but not good enough for any of you."

Sammy slammed his laptop closed, wrapped the cords around his free hand and shoved them into his computer case.

He turned to his sister. "So, Marnie will look after you. A woman rabbi. Is that any worse than what I'm doing? She... and her," he at gestured at Marnie and Tovah with venom in his eyes. "For women to make a living as a *Rav* is worse than anything I can do. It's *Hillul HaShem*, an affront to the Name. So let your lady rabbi look after you. Maybe she's not a prostitute, but our *Rav* wouldn't approve of her. That's for sure."

Sammy turned and, slamming the door of the hotel room after him. Eli could see the boy had left Tovah and Marnie badly shaken, and Liora crying.

CHAPTER NINETEEN

Bea and Walter Holland were once again pretending to spend the early morning as they usually did, reading the art sections of a stack of daily newspapers. For the last few days what they actually had been doing every morning was talking about their daughter.

Bea swept *The New York Times* off their glass topped patio table and let it fall to the floor where it ruffled in the wind, covering her feet in elegant straw-colored sandals, a perfect color match to her light khaki trousers.

Walter got up, leaving *The Los Angeles Times* spread out at his place. The wind picked it up and blew it all over the patio. Totally atypical for the Hollands, who were 'crazy neat' by their own admission, neither one of them paid any attention to the mess.

Walter stood at the edge of the patio kicking at the Plexiglas fence dividing the patio from the beach beyond. Bea joined him there.

"This is no good," she said, putting her hand over his. "We're not getting anything done, and, what's more, we're driving ourselves crazy. That girl!"

"Hardly a girl," Walter said. "Besides, this time I think she's found someone she likes."

"That doesn't sound so wonderful. The first time she went she found Shalom. We're still living with that disaster."

Bea marched back to the table; actually kicked the two newspapers on the patio aside and flung herself down into her chair. She poured herself a fresh cup of coffee, adding a huge dollop of hot milk and two sugar cubes. Walter knew that meant, 'to hell with my diet.'

He laughed. "You'll be eating chocolate pretty soon, and you'll blame Marnie for that too."

"She is to blame, for every extra pound and for every wrinkle."

"There isn't a wrinkle or an extra pound in sight," Walter assured her.

"You're lying like a rug," she said, "But I love you for it."

Walter sat down and picked up his coffee. He sipped, made a face. It was lukewarm. He picked up a piece of toast that had been spread with marmalade. He looked at it, considered biting into it, put it back on his plate.

"Okay," he said. "We're going to Israel."

"When would we do that?" Bea said. She thought he was kidding. She didn't move.

"We go ASAP, Bea. As you just said we're not getting anything done here. A day, maybe two. You ought to go pack. Keep it simple."

Bea knew one important thing about her easy-going husband. She knew exactly when he was not kidding.

She pushed back from the table, turning to go through the living room to the master bedroom.

The doorbell rang, and, at the same moment, the phone beeped. They looked at each other. "Door. You get the door," Walter said. "I'll take this." He picked up the phone.

"It's nothing," Bea said, "The dry cleaner pick-up, I'm sure." She headed for the door. As she crossed the 30-by-40 foot living room and the marble-floored foyer, she could see a man in a black suit and black hat through the leaded-glass window set into the door. She paused, took a deep breath and, pulling open the door, she said, "Well, as I…"

But her casual façade cracked and she said. "Shalom, why are you here? What do you want?"

At the same time, what she'd heard her husband saying as she left the patio, registered. "Hi, Kitten."

Walter was the only one who could call Marnie 'kitten' and live.

Shalom walked in, past his ex-mother-in-law. He sat down in one of a pair of exquisite living room armchairs, palest ivory with a crest motif in turquoise.

Shalom looked alien in the beautiful room, as though an extra-terrestrial had landed. Bea saw Walter slide the patio door shut. She sat down across from Shalom on a pale turquoise silk sofa.

Along with her unexpected guest, Bea watched as out on the patio Walter paced back and forth. For the moment neither Shalom nor Bea said a word. Bea didn't trust herself to speak, and it was clear Shalom was waiting for Walter.

Walter seemed to be almost inspired by what he was hearing on the phone. He spoke emphatically, waving his left hand, as though inscribing a huge arc. Bea knew he was responding to what Marnie was saying. There were a couple of quick interchanges between Walter and their daughter, then Walter spoke at length, he listened at length, then he hung up and came into the living room carrying the portable phone.

"Shalom," he said, "How odd. Marnie was just on the phone. You could have talked to her. She says there is a lot of monkey business going on in Jerusalem. Some of it is Sammy's, maybe some of it yours."

"Monkey business?" Shalom said, belligerence in every syllable. "What would be monkey business? My Sammy is not a monkey. I am not a monkey. Today I find out I am still married. I had a call from your lawyer, this morning at eight a.m."

Walter looked at his watch. "It's barely ten thirty. You made good time. I thought you'd gone to Indiana, but here you are. So Berman could reach you. How nice."

"I could not go to Indiana. My Katie, Chava's family, has said better not until my status is straightened out. Not that I will listen to them, but…. My status!!! I did nothing!! You…you did it all!!! Even Marnie would not be so…."

Walter sat down next to Bea, covering her hand with his. "You came here, you married my daughter. You married her according to the laws of this country. Why would I allow anything else? If you didn't know, that was your problem. You thought, you and your rabbi-friend thought, you had out-smarted me.

"By the way, Marnie isn't any happier to know about the marriage still existing than you are. So, what did the lawyer say, anyway?" Walter leaned forward. He wanted to know exactly how the conversation between Frank Berman and Shalom had gone.

"I must sign papers. I must agree to terms. Marnie will set terms!! That is not... it is not fitting for the woman to set terms. But if not, it goes to court for a hearing, and that will take too long," Shalom sputtered.

Walter leaned back, seeming so casual Bea was surprised Shalom didn't spring out of the chair and try to throttle her husband. As she watched, Shalom rubbed his clammy hands – she was sure they were clammy – up and down on the delicate fabric of her arm chair. This is a test, Bea thought. Let the bloody chair go hang. I'll have it reupholstered the moment we get back from Israel. Before that, even.

She would call her interior designer and order a new set of chairs; chairs in a totally different fabric. She might have to redecorate the whole room, to rid it of her memory of Shalom sitting in the armchair, rubbing his sweaty palms up and down. She swore she could see the stain he was creating, growing as they sat there.

Walter stood up. "According the Reverend Rabbi Dr. I. Schlumberger, who is my advisor on Jewish, Israeli and American marriage law, and with whom I've stayed in touch since you and Marnie were married – you will be bound by Marnie's terms. Every year I write him a check to help him continue his research into ancient texts on marriage. Fascinating subject. I believe he's going to dedicate his book on the subject to me and to Bea.

"Anyway, according to him, you have no choice. You set the terms for the *get*. Score one for you. Marnie gets to set the terms for the divorce. Score one, a big one, for our side. Your *get* was supposed to protect her, but you know that. Several thousand years have passed and you and some other orthodox men have debased the system. 'Debased,' that is the term Dr. Schlumberger uses. 'Debased.' His very word. He offered to put you in *cherem*, to excommunicate you, throw you out of Judaism, but he admits he'd have to let practically every orthodox rabbi in the world know what he's done. With modern travel it's impossible to keep track of you, to get them to forbid you to pray in a community, or eat with people, or work at a paying job. You have a business anyway, so you'd keep on running it. Sammy has a business too, I understand.

"Do you know Liora and Marnie are together now? They are both worried about these businesses, Sammy's and yours."

"Liora is with Marnie? I absolutely forbid that!" Shalom pounded his hand on the arm of Bea's beautiful chair. She felt like moaning. That chair was gone. That much was certain.

"It's not for you to forbid anything Marnie wants. She wants Liora with her. And, Shalom, if Frank Berman, an excellent lawyer by the way, says you need to agree to terms, you will. Rabbi Dr. Schlumberger says the same thing. You do know he is both a rabbi and a lawyer. Also, he holds a Yeshiva University PhD in Jewish studies. Brilliant man. So, the whole thing is totally out of my hands.

"Marnie told me. 'Dad, get it done. Get that divorce done. Then butt out. I mean it.'" she said.

"In fact she's so angry, I'm not sure who is going to get the worst of it, you or me. Of course I can't do much until she tells me what her terms are. So, I guess we both have to wait. But, Frank Berman will call her again. They've already spoken at least once. She just told me that."

Walter's gesture, hand outspread, palms up, suggested there was nothing he could do.

Shalom's face was turning redder by the minute. He's going to have a heart attack and die right here, Bea thought. That would solve a lot of problems.

Walter just continued on in a desultory way, despite Shalom's obviously increasing annoyance.

"She does have a friend helping her. Also, Liora is staying with her and Tovah for a few days. They've added a cot to their room. All those girls together; like a pajama party, I bet. They're all at the King David. She said it was just fine to tell you where she is. I suggest you call her. Do you need the number?" he asked helpfully.

Shalom stood up, looked at them both with loathing. "She will pay for this. You will pay for this."

"If you don't agree," Walter said, "You will pay for this, and your lovely fiancée too. I must call her father now that there are no secrets any more. He just did what I did so many years ago. He protected his daughter from a quickie marriage to a jerk, a marriage with no protection. He's a smart man.

"You should know that Dr. Schlumberger apologizes to me for your behavior every time we meet, every time we talk. 'It was never meant to be this way,' he assures me. In the ancient world, the system, it protected women. They got their dowry money back in a divorce.

"Not like you, asking an extra $20,000 to give Marnie the *get*. And keeping every penny I gave her before she was married. You kept her dowry. Definitely not allowed. God is good, I guess. Better than I expected. Oh, and I'm sure Dr. Schlumberger will assist your fiancée's family too. What did you say her real name was? Katie? She may never be Chava."

Shalom still stood there. Bea waited for him to kick the chair, or do something else equally loathsome, but he did not. He strode across the living room and foyer, pulled open the heavy front door, slamming it hard behind him. A few seconds later they heard his car accelerate out of their driveway.

"Okay, let's go Bea," Walter said. "Pack up. Tell the housekeeping service. Please put the home security company on notice.

"Damn, I wish we could go today, but we've got to set things up at work. That'll take a day, maybe two. Just remember to pack light. You can buy anything you need there. If we can leave by Wednesday, we can spend the night in New York and then fly New York to Ben Gurion. We'll need to be on that four-thirty flight. You can shop in Israel. You might be able to take Marnie shopping for a wedding dress in Israel, or in New York on the way back."

Bea looked up, "A wedding dress!! She told you she needs a wedding dress? She'd marry an Israeli? Not again! Does she even know we're coming?"

"No, he's an American. His name is Eli. Marnie was talking to me, Tovah and this Eli fellow at the same time, while I was on the phone. I even heard Liora. They heard about Sammy's business earlier. Not too cool, apparently. They're not happy, but they're trying to sort out whether Sammy might be with them if they can play it right, or if he'd be with his father. Marnie thinks probably he's only out for himself. Which, from what I've heard, seems to be the most likely.

"I heard a good five minutes of 'Eli, did you know...' and 'Eli, I need to tell my dad what we found on line.' 'Eli, do you agree?' That was Marnie.

"At the same time Tovah is saying, 'Good thing you're here, Eli.' I heard his voice too. Definitely an American. New York, I'd say. Anyway, I know what I know. Marnie doesn't have to tell me anything. And of course she doesn't know we're coming. Why would I tell her and give her an advantage?"

Bea could tell from Walter's grin that the dozen years he'd waited had been well worthwhile.

"I just hope Shalom doesn't decide to go back before we do," Walter continued. "Nah, that won't happen. He'll have to go to his maybe fiancée first, don't you think? Maybe to re-schedule the wedding?

"So, we'll just show up. Right now Marnie is kind of pissed with me, so, a little more or a little less, it won't matter much in the end.

"I can't understand why she's angry, anyway. For the first time in years she knows exactly where she stands, and she's got a guy. Not that she's actually told me about him.

"There's also that dig thing for her group for the next couple of days. If Shalom goes to Israel, or if he waits to phone her, he won't find her for a day or two. That might worry him enough to let Berman settle things quickly. I don't think Shalom will bother with an American lawyer of his own. He can't afford one, I'm sure.

"We need to set things up at the gallery before we take off. Day after tomorrow, first thing, we're off to New York and then Ben Gurion. Be ready, Bea."

CHAPTER TWENTY

The day after Sammy's visit to their hotel, Marnie faced the problem of what to do with a teenager, when a parent, the responsible adult, needs to be out of town.

Their class reunion was supposed to spend most of the next week at an archeological dig near a kibbutz in the north, at one of the many *tels* found in the area, returning right after Shabbat.

But, what to do with Liora? It was a long bus trip each way, in addition to the time at the dig. It meant the girl would be alone far too long for Marnie's peace of mind.

The girl argued, logically, that she was often at home alone and a hotel was probably safer than the Gasith home in Mea Shearim. But Marnie didn't want Liora to be alone. She wanted to spend time with her. She also wanted to see more of Eli, although the three of them, with and without Tovah, had shared most of their meals and spent hours and hours together.

Marnie also wanted to go with her classmates, at least for some time, to not always be the odd one out.

Marnie had seen how she'd hurt her classmates feelings when she had refused to come to the reunion in the first place. Apparently what she did mattered to these people.

But it seemed they also understood she had some responsibility for an orthodox teenage girl, and so would have to make her time with them much shorter. It appeared they respected her new responsibility, even if Marnie could see their confusion too.

"She's like family," Marnie said to anyone who brought up the subject of Liora.

She let them think it was a cousin or niece or something, some relation. She supposed that's what Liora was, or had been – a relative – in the broadest sense of the word.

Finally, in consultation with Eli, Tovah and Liora, they agreed a couple of nights alone would be okay. There was room service and Liora could have a girlfriend stay with her at least one night if she wanted company.

Eli would speed things up further by driving Marnie up and back. "We'll save a lot of time that way," Eli said.

The car ride was several hours faster than the bus, which had to make many stops along the way. Also, instead of staying at the dig, they would spend the nights in a hotel in Kiryat Shimona or Tiberius. Eli couldn't stay with the class anyway, so the hotel would be easier. Their plan gave Marnie great satisfaction. If you planned properly, you could arrange anything.

Early in the morning she and Eli waved to Liora as they left the King David parking lot. The girl had accompanied them down to the car. Eli wanted to complete their drive before the heaviest traffic and the heat of mid-day.

In addition to staying alone, Liora had agreed not to call her father or her brother, although there were no secrets any more. But, Marnie didn't want Liora bullied.

The girl had several shifts at work to put in. She had books and magazines to keep her busy. She loved watching television. She would be just fine. Everything was under control.

As they reached the outskirts of Jerusalem Eli reached across and took Marnie's hand. "Here's to our voyage of discovery," he said, squeezing her hand.

CHAPTER TWENTY-ONE

This trip will be like a vacation," Marnie said. "I know I'm supposed to be on vacation already, but somehow everything that's happened has made things too important to count as one."

They descended from the plateau of Jerusalem to enter the Jezreel valley, the breadbasket of Israel. Green fields sloped away in every direction, interrupted by orchards of fruit trees and ancient olive trees so gnarled it seemed impossible to believe they still provided bushels of olives every year.

"I had something quite different in mind than just a vacation," Eli said, taking Marnie's hand.

"Different?" Marnie felt as though she was just parroting, agreeing, although she didn't know with what. His hand was warm, his fingers interlaced with hers, an anchor.

"Time travel," he said. "A voyage of discovery."

"You mean you expect to discover something exceptional at the dig? I don't think it's really that kind of experience," Marnie responded.

"I don't know how much time we'll spend there," he said.

"If we don't get there, Tovah will worry."

"She won't worry. She knows you're with me, and I told her my plans; at least roughly."

"You told Tovah your plans, but not me?" Marnie didn't know whether to be amused or annoyed.

"She's easier to convince."

"Convince about what?"

Convince that the rest of your life, and mine is at stake. Since you're going home soon, we have very little time. That means we have to make time, compress time, find time. This is the trip where we do that."

"Eli, what are you talking about?" Marnie said, but a shiver ran through her. How odd that Eli should put what was going on in terms of time; the very thing she'd been obsessing about lately, although not sharing with anyone because it seemed so ungrateful.

She should be thinking about what she'd gained, not lost. But, she'd left a four-year-old and now there was a sixteen-year-old young woman willing to try to be her... Friend? Foster daughter? Well, perhaps what to call their relationship was premature. But she'd lost Liora's whole childhood, and probably lost Sammy totally.

Her anger with Shalom also focused on what he'd cost her in time; the years they'd been married and the years since. Some of the blame was her own. She'd declared she wouldn't marry again, that she wouldn't sign a *ketubah,* a Jewish marriage license again, giving all power to some man.

How did Eli know she was mourning lost time? She had barely admitted it to herself.

Eli seemed to have gathered a whole new level of resolve in the last day or two. Any quality of diffidence he'd once demonstrated was gone. He'd had his own demons, but had utterly defeated them. Was she some part of his victory?

Surely it was too dangerous to just let him take charge of her life, no matter what victory he was celebrating?

"I have a schedule for today and tomorrow," he said. "It doesn't really include the dig. I think we need to fold at least two months into the next couple of days."

"It doesn't include the dig? Then why are we going? I could have stayed with Liora. What two months?" Marnie was confused. Confusion always made her angry.

"We haven't known each other two months. We haven't known each other even two weeks?" Her heart was beating fast, and she could feel sweat trickling down her back bone and between her breasts.

"I thought we had decided it was important I spend some time with my classmates. They resented the idea I wasn't going to come at all, the fact I somehow excluded myself from their regular activities, I'd held myself aloof."

"Well, if you feel very strongly we could go by tomorrow and tell them why we couldn't get there."

"And why would that be?"

"I can't tell you yet," Eli said.

"Eli. You're not making sense!! Now you sound like my father. 'I couldn't tell you what I should have told you; because if I'd told you, it would have negated the very thing I was trying to protect you from by not telling you. And, I couldn't tell you, since you wouldn't agree.'"

"I bet you can't say that again," Eli said. He didn't seem rattled over Marnie questioning his plans. It was clear he felt he would prevail.

"How about this? You relax and when we get to lunch I'll tell you part of it" he said.

"Part! What part? This is like being kidnapped. What is it with you men, not telling me things?" Marnie was furious, flashing back on Shalom, his son, her father, even the lawyer who kept telling her they would look after everything.

"Hmm, you might have a point there. Okay, we can stop now and I'll tell you. I'm probably safe. We're already too far from Jerusalem for you to get out of the car and walk back."

Eli pulled the car over to the edge of the road and parked on the paved surface of the roadside. Paved to make sure no bombs were planted there, Marnie now knew. Turning to Marnie, he took her by the shoulders pulling her toward him, just as he had that first night in the car. Was he remembering the same moment?

"Think," he said. "The other night in the car, above Jerusalem, what did I say?"

His face was inches from her. He was going to kiss her. She wanted him to. But, she was angry, too. Could you be happy and angry at the same moment?

"You said to remember what you said. Not to forget it."

"What did I say?" How could he be so close and still not be kissing her?

"You said you loved…" The rest of it was lost in their kiss. One or the other of them, or both, had spanned the infinitesimal distance between them.

Finally they pulled apart. Seconds later? Minutes later? Marnie couldn't have said. She wasn't thinking clearly. When Eli talked about two months what could he mean? What two months? They would barely have two weeks in Israel before she had to go home.

It was all so serious for both of them, but, in moving away from her, Eli had banged his head hard on the windshield, lightening the moment considerably. Marnie giggled, than felt bad.

"Eli, I can say it now. I love you too. But that isn't a solution. It makes the problem bigger, worse."

"How can loving each other make things worse?" he said, rubbing his head.

"I love you. You love me," she said. "But, what can we do about it? You live here. I live in L.A. And worse, I'm married."

Still rubbing the side of his head where he'd smashed against the glass, Eli said, "It's time for us to decide things anyway. Never mind others' circumstances.

"When you were talking to your father yesterday, everything came together for me. I'm not willing to give that up. I'm not willing to give you up. I'll give up the *Yeshiva* if I have to."

"Eli, I couldn't let you do that. It's too important. The kind of teaching you want to do, it's revolutionary. Anyway, we can't decide things like this in a tiny parked car on some anonymous stretch of highway."

"I agree with you. That's what I've planned for, for the next two days. Oh, and by the way. We need a bigger car. We'll buy one before you go back to L.A. But right now what we are doing, is courting."

"Car? Courting?" There she was parroting again. A moment before she'd been questioning everything he said. What was wrong with her?

She shook her head as though to dislodge the echo she'd become. Then she thought: *Maybe I'm not parroting, maybe I'm agreeing. How can I? I'm still married.*

She repeated, "Eli, I'm still married."

"Doesn't matter," he said. He kissed her again, lightly this time, rubbed the tender spot on his head, straightened his pale blue *kippah* and pulled back onto the highway. "I've looked it all up. You and Shalom haven't lived together for years and years. Shalom will agree to your terms after he gets over being dictated to by a woman. His new wife may have a better hand to play because of it. So, maybe you're doing *a mitzvah*. She'll thank you one day. It's certain you'll get access to Liora, since that won't cost him anything. He'll bitch, but who cares? I'm sure Frank Berman has a judge he can coerce into a quickie divorce. Isn't California famous for that? It'll be fine.

"Anyway, we won't think about those details today. Today is for courting. Public dates as though we are *frum*. Then private time, as though we are modern. Courting at our age should normally take about two months. We're going to do it in two days. That's all the time we have."

"Two months in two days? Is that what you mean?" She knew where courting usually ended.

She moved on to what she could address. "You want us to act as though we're modern, and, as though we're *frum?* If we don't know which, how can anyone else?"

Eli took his hands off the wheel, turned to her. She flapped her hands at him. "Drive," she said. "Watch the road."

"I can steer this way," he said. He seemed to be steering the car with his left knee.

"Don't you see? It doesn't matter. We are our own unique category?" Eli leaned back, triumphant. "I finally figured that out."

"You want it both ways? Is that the point you're trying to make? No. You actually want it all ways! I don't think you can do that." Marnie laughed for moment, but then she stopped. "Can you?"

Eli put both hands back on the wheel, thumping it once, for emphasis. "I'm right. You can. We can. We've been trying... well we haven't been admitting to anything, 'cause it was so early, 'cause we just met,' 'cause of Liora.' I can think of a million reasons. But they don't count. Not any of them.

"Marnie, we've been playing this as though we are shy virgins; as though a *shatchan* set us up and we're following the rules for the 'getting to know you' dates for orthodox youngsters. But we're grown up. We need to chart our own lives."

"It's hard," Marnie said. "We don't have much time, and the conference is so public. Plus, Liora is a reality. I don't want to be a bad example to her. It's hard for her. We're so different. And, I want her around."

Marnie took a fresh water bottle Eli handed her and took a sip. "Then there's Tovah of course."

"Tovah wants you to go slow? I don't believe it." Eli took the water bottle out of her hand.

"Do you mind if I share?" he said. A husband, a lover, would do that, Marnie thought. She flushed, watched him finish the bottle of water, crunch the plastic in his hand and add it to trash bag on the back seat. That's what he already thinks he is.

"No, it's quite the opposite, with Tovah. How can she be so certain we ought to…?" Marnie couldn't go on. It was too blatant, too close to what she really wanted. Too close to the erotic dreams she'd been having. It was all too adolescent.

"Has she mentioned what we ought to do?" Eli moved over, put one arm around Marnie, pulled her close again, and kissed her, not banging his head again, and not watching the road. He kissed her deeply, thoroughly.

It flashed through Marnie's head that no teenage boy had ever driven one-handed with his arm around her. She ought to enjoy her version of the experience.

"Now, on we go" he said. He actually had his attention back on the road. Thankfully there had not been much traffic. He had controlled the car with his knee and had used his left hand to smooth her hair back from her forehead.

"So beautiful," he said about her, as though he'd received some small bonus, not important, but very nice to have.

"All this was meant to be a romantic lunch discussion, not something exchanged in a hot car while driving. But I guess we'll find something else to talk about. Without knowing it you've moved the schedule up. I figure we gained a week at least."

Marnie didn't argue his calendar any further. With her own hand she traced where his hand had been on her forehead. Where his kiss had been. Could two people really make up their own categories, their own rules, their own calendar?

"Of course, if you told Tovah to drown me, or throw me off the top of the Shalom Tower, because it would help our relationship, she'd do it. Maybe that would also speed up your calendar?" She thought that might get a response. It didn't though, except for a smile.

"I've never seen anything like it. No one can tell Tovah what to do, or when to do it. Not even her husband. But with you, it's 'Yes, Eli,' and 'Sure, Eli.' So help me, it's like I've been handed over to you."

"Do you object?"

"Well, no. But Tovah of all people; not putting up an argument. It's very weird."

Marnie leaned against the door, took the fresh water bottle Eli handed her. She took a sip.

"She knows what's good for you. That's all. She believes in your happiness. And mine, too, for that matter. We both deserve to be happy."

That idea silenced Marnie. "I've never thought about life in those terms," she said, soberly. "Being happy. It's never even occurred to me."

"Well, it's allowed. The point is, all the rules – don't touch, don't be alone – make no sense for us. Neither of us wants to get married under the system. We don't even want to have a serious relationship under those rules. I'm not going to wreck a hotel room, not even a guest house, and you're not going to run away with a scholar, because he's orthodox and therefore safe."

"Eli," Marnie whispered. "I'm still married."

"Yes, you are married. You keep saying that. And I can understand how you feel. But, oddly, that clarifies your life. For the first time we know it, so we know what Shalom wants. You want the same, with a few details added. Also, for the first time you have an effective weapon against him. You've connected with Liora, and you'll count in her life, no matter what happens. Even Sammy might come around. You may have threatened your parents with mayhem, but they didn't do anything except try to protect you. It worked, too. When you didn't know you were married, you were fighting the very idea of a relationship. Your dad made his own rules about how to handle a bad marriage. We can make our own rules too."

"That seems like such *chutzpah*. We make up our own rules, we go our own way. It didn't…" Marnie was trying to clarify how she felt and not succeeding very well.

Eli had no such problems. "Don't you see? Most of our life we've been working against the rules. Maybe that's just the way we are. Trying and failing to follow the rules brought us here today.

"You and I are so gun-shy about our earlier relationships we both got stuck in some kind of cul-de-sac in time. Time needs to run forward for both us again. We're not going to do anything outrageous. We're going to have profound respect for each other. We're just going to figure out what works for the two of us."

Eli took the water bottle out of Marnie's hand. He didn't ask this time, just glugged the water down, as though he needed it to finish his thought.

"We're two rabbis, unusual in and of itself. We're two rabbis in a country that doesn't recognize you, and isn't totally certain about me. Neither of us is orthodox, but we live a life style that could be interpreted as sort of orthodox. So how can the regular rules apply? You said Dan and Tovah had to hash things out in a different way, to make their marriage work. You said they had a rough spot some years ago. Right?

"Yes, right. But Eli, I shouldn't even think of a relationship until the lawyers work out things with Shalom."

"Wrong. Your parents know what needs to be done and it's been set in motion. You have a weapon to use against Shalom. You can move on. Remember what I said: I love you. Remember what you said: you love me. That was our starting point for today. We've already moved on to the next stage."

After their morning on the road, they entered the northern upland areas of Israel, the Galilee. Eli insisted on circling the lake before driving to Tiberius, a city named for the Roman Caesar who had first built a villa there.

Marnie's first glance of Lake Kinneret from the Golan Heights was thrilling, the harp shape giving the lake its Hebrew name beautiful and so obvious.

The Sea of Galilee restaurant on the shore carried the Christian version of the name of the lake. Eli pulled in there.

"We're stopping for lunch," he declared. He went around to the other side of the car to open Marnie's door for her.

Marnie found Eli very focused on a schedule he'd created. Lunch on the outdoor patio above the shining lake, sheltered by a large, blue and red Cinzano umbrella was magical. It reminded her of that first conversation they'd had while waiting to see Liora and Sammy.

At that first meeting neither of them had known why the other was at the Mea Shearim corner café. Who could have guessed where that first meeting would lead?

She knew she would remember this day just as well as she remembered the Mea Shearim café, the day she and Eli came to know each other so intimately. Was that the day Eli's calendar had begun?

She had used the word 'intimate' in her own thoughts. It was almost as though Eli read her mind and felt the same. He had no more secrets to share, but after lunch, when Marnie laid one hand on the table, Eli took it in his, caressing it, turning it palm up to kiss the softest part of her wrist.

In addition to their lunch stop, Eli had arranged for a tour of Tiberius in a horse-drawn carriage.

At first the driver paralleled the city's most popular tourist area, a kind of boardwalk. Eli gestured toward it with his one free hand.

"The boardwalk itself is too touristy for us today, so we will do that next time," Eli said. "Today we'll do the Jewish sites and a few other spots."

It was four-thirty by the time they had visited the sites Eli had in mind. To Marnie's way of thinking, he'd left the best for last, the tomb of the great scholar Maimonides. Marnie didn't want to pray there particularly, but the fact that a scholar whose work she saw every time she opened a volume of Talmud, the commentator of commentators, was buried there, filled her with awe.

"The people who come here often pray for fertility or a marriage partner," Eli said. "Like the bracelet."

At one of the stops he bought her a red-ribbon bracelet, a popular amulet. She knew it was a fertility symbol, but neither of them believed in such a thing, so where was the harm in wearing a little memento?

They had been driven around a good portion of the lake, then doubled back to enjoy the sunset.

"This is an equal-opportunity tour," Eli joked. "Jesus walked on the waters of that lake and, up there," he pointed to the Mount of the Beatitudes, "is where he delivered the Sermon on the Mount."

"I love it all," Marnie agreed. "I know Tovah loves Tiberius too. Does she know we're here?"

"She knows our schedule exactly. There's no point in joining them now, just for dinner. We'll go and get settled instead. Not at a hotel, though. That's not the best place up here in the Galilee. I've made reservations for a guest house at Kibbutz Snir. It's right next to Tel Dan, near the dig. However, it isn't kosher, so I brought our own supplies."

Marnie had seen a large cooler in the back of the car, but didn't know why Eli had brought it along.

Marnie was feeling cosseted, relaxed, protected. This was proving to be one of her first real tourist outings in Israel.

She had lived in Israel during the first year of rabbinical school and before, when she was married to Shalom. But she had never seen much of Israel. Shalom thought being a tourist '*narishkeit*,' foolishness, a waste of time.

"Thank you for this day," she said to Eli. They were hand-in-hand, as they had been all day.

✡

Kibbutz Snir was only a half hour drive from Tiberius, uphill all the way. As they pulled into the kibbutz, Eli pointed out the road they would take tomorrow.

"The dig is only a few miles in that direction. If we get everything on our schedule done, we can drop in on our way home."

"Get everything done?" Marnie was back to parroting.

She was going to laugh but something in Eli's expression stopped her.

"I'm figuring week four, maybe a little further," Eli said. He was making Marnie very nervous so she turned back to marvel at their view of Mt. Hermon's snow-capped top, eight thousand feet above them. She seemed to have committed herself to whatever Eli had in mind. There was no point in arguing now.

Kibbutz Snir had been founded by Americans who had turned the garden-like settlement into a paying proposition. "They've got avocados and bananas," Eli said, "But you have to experience some of the gardens the *kibbutzniks* have set up. They've got stands of papyrus and bamboo that are growing farther north than anywhere else in the world. And then there are the hedges."

Eli tugged a handful of sprigs from one of the groomed bushes lining every sidewalk and deployed decoratively around every low building.

"Sniff," he said. The fragrance of rosemary engulfed Marnie. "Rosemary is a major tea and spice product here. There's nothing like standing near the hedges at night."

When the two of them left the kibbutz's small check-in facility, Marnie carried her overnight bag and Eli *shlepped* his own small duffle bag and rolled the wheeled refrigerator-like cooler he'd stored in the back of the car and had plugged into the cigarette lighter.

Where could they be staying? Would it be in one of the little houses scattered around the area?

They were walking through a district two city blocks long where there were no buildings. The sidewalk seemed to dead-end right into one of the largest, most heavily-leafed tree Marnie had ever seen.

"So we're staying in that tree? In a tree house?" she asked.

"Yep, right in that tree," Eli said and he walked right into the center of the huge tree under some of the bower-like branches that had been trimmed to just head height. Everywhere else, along the tree's circumference, the branches swept the ground.

'It's a fig tree," he said. "The biggest I've ever seen. I always figured this had to be the fruit of the tree of good and evil that Adam and Eve ate from. Who would have bothered for an apple? But figs, now that's another story. Probably well worth any sin or whatever knowledge they gained."

There, near the center, in the natural clearing around the tree's thick trunk, were two tiny cottages, one room each. There was also a stone pit for a fire, a picnic table with two benches and a huge hammock slung between the trunk and the side of one of the houses.

Unless you'd visited before you'd never have known there was anything at all snuggled under the huge tree. The whole setting was magical. Elves or hobbits came to mind, not matter-of-fact kibbutzniks, or romantic tourists.

"One house each?" she said, feeling odd questioning his plans.

But her comment didn't seem to bother him. "One each," he agreed. "With a patio between them, so we can eat some supper and really talk."

It was dark by then, but the guest houses had lighting. The two of them were sheltered, utterly alone, protected by the huge tree and by the surrounding dark, made more intense by the tree.

The tree would be a character in the personal story the two of them were creating. Marnie would never forget this tree.

A half hour later Marnie and Eli were sitting opposite each other at the food-laden picnic table between the two houses. Around them insects chirped and whistled, but other than that it was still.

"I know this is supposed to be about the dig for your class," Eli said. "But we have to talk. We have to move things along. This seemed to be the only time. I'm hoping you might stay longer in Israel, maybe an extra week." He put his hand up, to still her objections. "We can deal with that later, though. It's not absolutely necessary.

"You and I have been circling each other ever since we met. Since I took your phone number. Since I tried to *schmear* sun block on you.

"To save my life, you said." Marnie said, still amused.

"To save my life too," Eli said. He reached across the table and took Marnie hand. "And it did."

CHAPTER TWENTY-TWO

Marnie was wondering what might come next, and where they might be in Eli's two-month calendar, when the cell phone she was using in Israel rang. At practically the same moment Eli's phone also rang.

They looked at each other. Their precious privacy had suddenly been invaded. They had seemed suspended in an all-protective, Eden-like space, if only for this one night. But, the world was still out there.

Phones in hand, they each reported on who was calling. "Liora," Marnie said, panicky, and, at the same time, Eli said, "It's the front desk at the hotel. I told them to call me if anything happened."

On the phone Liora was very calm despite the fact Marnie could hear several loud male voices, one of them Sammy's, in the background.

Eli was reporting, "The front desk says that a young man has just gone upstairs, with one of their senior security men, insisting that his sister has to come home with him. His father called from the States, apparently from Indiana, and says his daughter does not have his permission to be at the King David."

At the same moment Liora said to Marnie, in as crisp a delivery as she'd ever heard from the girl, "Please tell Eli that my brother is trying his tricks, so Eli has to use the papers we signed and the money I gave him. As we agreed, he's to please phone to my uncle. Right now. I think Sammy called the police. Tell Eli right now! I'll hang on."

Marnie, feeling more like the child than the adult in the exchange turned to Eli. "You and Liora arranged something, papers, money, a call to her uncle. What?"

Eli waved a hand at her and listened for another second. "Aha, the police are there. Good. Put him on. Oh, her. Even better. Yes, *Samal Sheni.*

In an aside to Marnie: "Good, they sent a woman sergeant, better than just a corporal."

Then, almost without time for the police sergeant to speak, Marnie heard enough to figure out the story Liora and Eli had created.

"*Samal Shani,* thank you for looking in on my student.

"As you can probably tell, her family objects to her getting an education. They would not let her attend high school, but, she feels she must attend, and then do national service, if she is to be a part of modern Israel.

"Yes, the seminary will let her complete high school, first thing. She has already arranged it. She will begin with the new semester. Her stepmother has housing for her until the dormitory is open. Her uncle is sending papers, as the manager at the front desk told you.

"Yes, she is sixteen. Of course she is sixteen. Otherwise I couldn't do this. Yes, I've been paid. And her uncle has authority anyway. He's in Beersheva.

"He's not so good with modern technology, but I'm sure he'll find a fax by tomorrow.

"Right, yes, he speaks Hebrew, so you can certainly call him. Polish, too, if you have someone...

"Okay, you'll wait for the papers by fax. That's good. Yes, her father is in the States and her brother has moved out of the family home. They already left her alone many times. She runs their office and works at a *gan* in the German colony.

"Yes, I'm the *Rosh* of my *Yeshiva*.

"Yes, tuition is all looked after. Yes, and a home for her. Yes."

Then he listened more patiently. The policewoman on the other end was going upstairs. Eli waited, briefing Marnie.

"She's clearing Sammy and the men with him out of Liora's room, and has had the hotel change the keys, and add some extra security. Liora has called a friend from the *gan* to come and stay with her. The police sergeant says the girl is remarkable, calm and self-possessed. Is that what you would say?"

"Liora?" Marnie was ready to quiz the girl.

But Liora was way ahead of her. "*Ima Malka*, I'm fine.

Marnie felt a catch at her heart, in her breath, at 'Ima Malka' coming so naturally from Liora.

"Eli and I planned for this, honest. My friend Galit will be here in ten minutes. We will use room service. I will rent a movie for us. Sammy cannot bother me again. Honest, I'm fine. You stay where you are. I'll see you tomorrow; no, the day after. But my father is not in L.A. any longer. He is with his *bashert* in Indiana now. They will come here soon. Eli has papers and some money, a token, from me. He has my uncle's phone number, who has other emergency papers that *Abba* left with him long ago. I am sixteen now. It's of age for many things. Do not worry."

Then, suddenly the totally in-control young woman Marnie was speaking to crumbled. Liora giggled and then broke down in tears. Her English deserted her for a minute too. "*S'lichah,*" she said.

"Don't say 'I'm sorry.' You have nothing to be sorry for," Marnie said. "You're doing great. Take a minute, catch your breath."

Liora was back to giggling. "*Rak Rega,*" she said, colloquially, 'wait a minute,' something you heard everywhere in Israel.

All in all, it only took Liora a minute or two to regain the calm she'd lost. Marnie heard the girl put down the phone, blow her nose, then she returned to their conversation. The triumphant young woman was back. "It's good to plan. It was exciting."

"And, maybe just a little scary?" Marnie observed.

"Maybe a little," Liora agreed. "But worth it. It really is. Ah, the phone is beeping. That will be Galit. I'll phone you tomorrow morning." Liora clicked off.

Marnie's restless pacing while she spoke on her phone brought her close to the giant hammock. It had to be at least ten feet long. It was slung high off the ground. With great care, she sat down on the edge of it, in the middle, letting it rock her to and fro a little. She was suddenly exhausted, although the whole episode had lasted less than ten minutes. How had Eli known Sammy would make a move? How had he known what to do in advance?

All she could think was to ask Eli as she tried to smile, "Was this on your calendar?"

Eli was standing over her. "No, it didn't have an official spot on the timeline. But I thought it might. I checked. Liora can't vote, and there's no legal drinking age, so that's not an issue. She can get married, and she can leave school. She's of age for a lot of things in Israel. The police think she's of age at sixteen, especially if her older brother and father are out of the country or have left her in charge, alone at work. Her uncle has papers saying he can be responsible for medical emergencies, things like that. Shalom was smart to do that. But in this case, it caught him out. It's as though he gave his uncle permission to make decisions. And the old man thinks a *frum yeshiva*, paid for, a girls' seminary or high school, is just the thing for his niece."

"You're not a girls' seminary!" Marnie had to protest.

"Did I say she was going to my school? We'll find somewhere for her, mine, or someone else's, what's the difference? And a family she can board with. I'll pay for it, or you'll pay for it. Something."

"You're something," Marnie said weakly. She was trying to smile. Eli had accomplished so much. Liora was safe and freer then she'd been. But Marnie's smile didn't make it all the way to her lips. Or if it did, the tears in her eyes confused her message.

"Oh, honey, don't cry. I know, it was scary, but only for a minute. Sammy wasn't going to get anywhere. Liora wasn't going with him anyway. She had the police on speed dial. The hotel manager knew all about it. I tipped every bellman, every desk clerk. She was safe, so safe."

Eli dropped down beside Marnie, putting his arms around her. The hammock rocked violently under his weight and his height overbalanced them. Over she went with him, the two of them getting completely enfolded in the mesh of the hammock.

"This wasn't on the calendar either," Eli said as they rocked back and forth. "But I think I'll add it, right now."

CHAPTER TWENTY-THREE

There the two of them were cocooned in a mesh nest, in the deep quiet of the space under their amazing fig tree. Apparently everyone Marnie might worry about was safe and quiet, or too far away to make any trouble, at least for this night. Her class was nearby on their dig. Her parents and their lawyer were in California getting the divorce that Marnie hadn't known she'd needed until a few days ago. There were problems, immediate problems, but there was someone else, someone who loved her, to help look after them. She could feel the stress lift, an actual sensation of release off her shoulders.

Sammy had been routed from the King David by a woman police sergeant and Eli's minion of paid-off hotel employees. Shalom and his fiancée, his '*bashert*' as Liora insisted on calling the poor girl who was going to marry Shalom and become his fifth wife, were far away in Indiana.

Even if Shalom and Katie – Chava – were planning to travel to Israel, they wouldn't leave until after Shabbat.

Fate, God, something had tipped her into the arms of this tall, redheaded man, a fellow rabbi, a rebel it seemed, who had a total disregard for any of the normal rules of courtship. The only sensible plan was to learn to relax and enjoy being looked after.

The two of them had been swinging gently back and forth for a while. Eli had both his arms very nicely around her. She had managed to work one arm more or less free, but there seemed nothing else to do with it other than wrap it around Eli's mid-section.

"Are you cold?" he wanted to know.

"No, are you?"

"No, but I'm surprised."

"Surprised?"

"You're not fighting to get out of this thing"

Eli plucked at some of the strands of the hammock he could reach. They thrummed a little, like a guitar. He seemed to be able to create a tune with them.

"Would fighting this thing work?" she wondered in an idle tone of voice. She was resting in his arms and her head was nestled nicely into his shoulder. One of her arms was kind of compressed between them.

She waggled her head slightly. "Is my head going to make your arm numb?"

"I suppose it might, in three or four hours. But I wouldn't worry about it now." His other hand was free to soothe her. He had somehow worked it under her t-shirt and it was moving up and down her spine, warm, quite lovely.

"So it's not logical, that's why you're not fighting the hammock?" he inquired.

"There doesn't seem to be much point," Marnie observed. "Besides, you probably have some plan for getting me to stay here. Maybe tacks on the ground. Perhaps, stealing my shoes. Some other kind of system to grab me, wrap me up. I couldn't even guess about your plans for Liora, so I'm sure I have no idea of what you might have in mind for me. I take it we're at the private time of your calendar, grown-up courting. Was it supposed to be even more private than this?"

She moved her free hand up and down his back, feeling the muscles bunch then relax as her hand glided over them. Her other hand, between them, wasn't free to do much else except move against the buttons of his shirt, opening them one after another, until her hand was resting against his bare chest.

On a quick intake of breath Eli said, "I didn't plan this part in too much detail. If the phone call from Liora didn't come we'd still be sitting at the picnic table. We didn't get as far as dessert."

"Dessert would have been nice, I suppose. What did you have in mind?" She nuzzled her head further in toward his chest, planting one light kiss, then another, on the part of his chest she could reach.

"Did I miss a step?" Eli breathed. "This is as good as dessert. I don't know that we ought to…"

Somehow he moved his shoulder and arm enough to bring her face up to his and kissed her long and sweet, tightening his hold on her at the same time. Marnie was certainly not going to fight those kisses, the intense pleasure that coursed through her body. She had never felt this way before.

'I don't think we ought to either," she agreed, but you did say 'dates as though we're modern and alone.' I don't think…this kind of…canoodling, I think they used to call it, necking, is so out of bounds if we're alone. What do you think, Rabbi?"

"Given the locations we pick, a miniscule Fiat and a somewhat restrictive hammock, we're probably safe from getting totally out of line. In the interests of research and propriety, we can see how far we can take things. What do you think?"

Someday, Marnie thought, *we'll have to tell our children about this. They'll never believe it. A small car and a very large hammock kept us relatively innocent while we were courting. The two of us: an almost divorced woman with a disastrous first marriage behind her, and a rock star who had too many groupies, who still feels guilty about exploiting them. So, if it kills us, we're going to behave.*

She and Eli, wrapped in each other's arms, some kissing, some caressing, a great deal of loving, eventually fell asleep in their net cocoon, spending the night there.

CHAPTER TWENTY-FOUR

arnie woke the next morning to the heavenly fragrance of coffee.

"Does this tree also grow coffee beans," she mumbled, eyes still closed. Where was Eli?

"I untangled myself much earlier, got us some blankets, came back to bed, er, hammock, and more recently visited the dining hall. There's fresh coffee, fresh yoghurt, fruit and cereal."

Marnie peeled open one eye. "I can't see a thing," she complained.

"You're facing the wrong direction," Eli observed. He provided a strong arm, pulled her, gently, out of the hammock where he'd covered her with a thin blanket. He pointed her toward the table between the two guest houses. Somewhere along the line, she'd lost most of her clothes, which seemed to have ended up under the hammock. She still had enough clothes to claim some modesty. She pulled the blanket around her, sarong style.

"There are showers and a bathroom in there." He pointed helpfully. "Towels and soap, everything you'll need. Even a hair dryer. Coffee first, or clean up first?"

"Shouldn't we be very uncomfortable with each other? Very self-conscious?" Marnie asked. She put her arms around Eli and leaned her head against his bare chest. His skin was slightly damp from his shower. He was wearing what she now knew were his favorite pair of faded blue jeans, almost white with age. He was holding a pale blue polo shirt, the same shirt he'd worn the day she'd met him and, as usual, his pale blue *kippah* was perched on his head. No one had made it for him. The sales girl in some store had said it was a good color for him. She'd thought it matched his eyes.

"Why?" he asked. "We managed to get a good month and a half into my calendar, I figure. By now we'd be past self-conscious. Let's get out of here, drive past the dig and go home. We have a teenager in Jerusalem waiting for us. If we'd met when we were in our early twenties, she could be ours. Well, yours. I wasn't a responsible human being until about seven years ago."

"She was just past two when I married Shalom, still a baby really. I was nineteen. Even on my accelerated schedule I was a little young. But I'm not now, and neither are you."

Picking up the clothes she found lying on the ground under the hammock she retreated to the guest house. Twenty minutes later, showered, shampooed, and properly dressed, she sat across from Eli at the picnic table.

"Liora called while you were in the shower," Eli reported. "She's fine. She's on her way to work. She's also checked the office: emails and so on. Everything is fine. She's going to try to talk to Sammy, but she doesn't know if he'll talk to her. Either way, she doesn't expect any trouble. He isn't staying at the house, but she'll go and check on it. She'll expect us very late tonight. You don't need to call her."

They were finishing breakfast and their second cups of coffee when Marnie asked, "A month and half into your calendar. No further?"

"We're stuck here for a while. You are still married, as I'm happy to say you haven't mentioned for hours. But it's a barrier, so we need to stand still for a while. That's okay. There's a lot to do at this juncture."

Marnie was enjoying Eli's unique approach to what he quaintly called courting.

"Such as?"

"Meet the parents. Figure out who will marry us. How will we manage a two-country life? More complex even then bi-coastal. Could it be a problem? That is after I feel free to ask you. Or, if you prefer, you could ask me. I'm not hung up on that, at all. Or, we can just agree that we're going to do it the minute it's appropriate. What do you think?"

Marnie had swallowed the wrong way and was choking on her coffee. It went down part way, and then came up more or less the same path, plus her nose, spraying all over both of them.

"Ugh," was all she could get out, besides coughing.

"If I laugh, you'll kill me, right?"

Not able to speak yet, Marnie just nodded, got up and ran for the guest house. Ten minutes later she was back, having changed her clothes again.

"Don't ever do that again," she said. "You think I'm supposed to ask you to marry me?"

"Oh, I'll do it, happily. I just didn't want to preempt you. You said something like that last night. We should be together forever, you said. Sounded like a proposal to me."

CHAPTER TWENTY-FIVE

Later Marnie realized, if waking up in a hammock after one of the most passionate nights of your life with the man you're going to marry is a surprising way to start the day, you can be forgiven for not believing there will be more surprises before the day ends.

The reactions of their friends and colleagues at the archeological dig on the next kibbutz were certainly a surprise. At least, she was surprised. Eli seemed to expect the reaction. Marnie would never have thought there'd be such a noticeable difference in how people treated her.

She'd looked in the mirror in the morning. Yes, she felt different. Eli had made a huge change in her life. But, she didn't think the change was obvious.

Was it because she and Eli had almost completed his two-month calendar of courting in a mere twenty-four hours? Did people sense that? Certainly neither she nor Eli had actually said anything about their personal calendar.

When they showed up at the *tel,* the smiles greeting them indicated everyone knew there was something new in their lives. Other than their courting behavior, what could it be? How did everyone recognize it?

Marnie was trying for dignity, as though showing up with a 'boyfriend'–– 'boyfriend' sounded juvenile but it seemed like the only appropriate term – was something she did all the time.

No matter who caught her eye, from Tovah down to people on the dig she didn't even know, everyone assumed Eli was right beside her. And there he was, never more than a few steps away.

Then, whoever spotted them smiled, as though they knew exactly what was going on between the two of them. Obviously their relationship had been a topic of discussion, without anyone knowing about their tree, the guest houses or the huge hammock.

It didn't help that she and Eli always seemed to be about to touch each other, or to have just touched each other. She'd never been so aware of anyone before. It wasn't deliberate. It just seemed to work out that way. Either he'd just have offered her his arm or hand to help her over some rock or pile of mud, or she, wanting to show him something, would put her hand on his arm, or his shoulder. Especially if he was squatting in front of her, looking at some aspect of the dig.

Once she pushed his *kippah* back on his head. He had been leaning over a ditch, talking to one of the archeologists, and the skullcap was slipping. She didn't want him to lose it. It was his favorite, and, although he used a clip, it often didn't hold. Without thinking, she just re-centered it on his head, and adjusted the clip, only to look up and see several of her classmates, led by her very best friend Tovah, looking at her as though she'd just done something extra brilliant. They were all smiling at her in a certain way.

Well, she wasn't ever going to do it again. Except when Eli stood up, he reached for his *kippah*, readjusted it minutely, said, 'Thanks', and tapped her gently on the nose. Did people do such things to each other often, she wondered? Or, was it only when they were in the middle, or at the end, of a period of courting.

After he'd tapped her on the nose – it was a loving gesture, she could tell – he took her by the shoulders and spun her around so they were both heading for the dining hall. He took her hand as they walked to the hall and led her to a table so they could sit together. The tables had long benches on each side. He'd continued to hold her hand, aiding her balance while she clambered over a bench. He'd also offered Tovah a hand, so she could sit on his other side. To Marnie it seemed Eli had made an equal opportunity gesture of helpfulness to Tovah. But, offering his hand to Tovah made no impression on anyone.

She was going to have to learn not to blush. Could you learn not to blush? It was probably one of those troublesome autonomic things; you couldn't help it. You probably had to de-sensitize yourself by doing something over and over again. That wasn't going to help much, since she was only going to be in Israel a few more days.

Plus, Eli kept looking after her. He passed her every single dish on the table. All the food was served family style and the midday meal wasn't really lunch, it was dinner.

So there was soup, meat, potatoes and rice, and lots of cooked vegetables. Plus there were all sorts of pickles and other side dishes on the table: fresh pita, tiny pickled white eggplants, cucumber and onion salad, hummus and sweet red pepper and tomato salad. Eli put some of that right on her plate without even asking.

"I know you love this stuff," he said. "Salad Turqie." Everyone at their table smiled at him, just as they had at her when she fixed his *kippah*.

All Marnie could think to say, since she knew she was blushing again, was, "Thanks. It's delicious."

His answer, "It sure is," seemed to be fraught with meaning.

Thankfully all this stopped when everyone had a siesta right after the mid-day meal, in a big tent full of army cots, made breezy with huge fans.

After avoiding the worst of the sun, those at the dig would work the rest of the day into the cool of the evening, only stopping for supper when it got dark.

After their naps she and Eli left for Jerusalem.

"It's relatively cool today," Eli said as he pulled the car out onto the highway.

"It will be much warmer as we go lower down. We're going to be driving through heavier traffic than when we came north, so we won't try to rush it. We'll stop for supper if we get hungry or too tired."

"That was a lot of dinner. We'll probably be able to wait," Marnie said. "We've got water and snacks too. Tovah seems to think we'd starve in the car if we went more than an hour or two without provisions. What is it with her, anyway?"

"She's helping me look after you. And the other way round, too. She thinks neither of us has a lot of experience in allowing others to take the load."

"Even now? She knows I was married before, and with your background?"

"Well, those experiences were different. It's like equating my groupies with a *shiddach* date like Liora. Not the same thing. Both of us have such unconventional histories. This is unique in a whole new way. I'm happy to have her help keep it this way."

Eli put his arm around her shoulders, pulled her close in beside him, kissed her on the side of her face, ruffled her hair and said. "Relax." As he drove, his long fingers began beating out some kind of percussive tune on the steering wheel.

"I swear, I could write music again," and he began to hum and count out a beat something like one of the wordless tunes, *niggunim*, rabbis often used when they were going to pray or sing at the beginning of synagogue services: "di di, di diddle di diddle, di…" a 'warm-up' tune played by a *klezmer* group.

"Do you want me to drive, so you can write that down," Marnie offered. Whatever he was humming, beating out and mouthing, sounded pretty good to her.

"No, I'll remember," he said. "I think there might be a lot more music now." He smiled at her so broadly, so happy, so handsome. She wondered how she'd ever thought he was gawky or awkward. Eli, somehow combined with Rattler – he kept insisting that was what had happened to him in the last few days – was more relaxed, certainly more musical, and much more handsome. She wasn't sure how this joining had come about, but she believed him. She didn't need any proof. She could see it in Eli's manner, face and body posture.

"You'll write wonderful music," she predicted.

"Yes, we will."

"We? Not you and me, certainly. I'll applaud."

"We. You applauding, me and Rattler."

"There are two of you? Three of us, counting me?"

"Not any more. I think I'm just one, now." Eli said. He paused, looked thoughtful, but his fingers were still tapping out a beat on the steering wheel and on Marnie's shoulder.

"Yep. The two parts of me have become one. So, with you, that's two. Like two rhythms but they become one song. Maybe that's like a marriage; two people become one marriage. A good drummer can do several things at once; but when it's heard along with everyone else playing, it's one piece of music."

"Are you sure you don't want to write that down?" Marnie said. "The music and what you just said. My head is spinning a little. Won't you forget something?"

Marnie turned her head to confirm that his fingers on her shoulder were doing something quite different from his fingers on the steering wheel.

"Do you forget a Talmud argument once you have it?" he asked.

"No. Not if it's good; and certainly not if it's new."

"Exactly," Eli said. "That's it exactly. I've got this, and it's good, and new. I won't forget."

With Eli's music thrumming in his hands and through their bodies, Eli wheeled the car into the King David parking lot. Marnie listened; her heart and mind open to Eli's new and wonderful music as they drove to where Liora was waiting for them.

CHAPTER TWENTY-SIX

The days after Marnie and Eli returned from the dig were some of the most peaceful and productive of Marnie's stay in Israel. Not to say she didn't have things to think about and problems to solve.

But her problems were actually enjoyable. Hard to believe that which school Liora would attend – Eli had found at least three to choose from – made for such meaningful discussion among the three of them. It took two dinners to make a choice.

There was their wedding to think about. The two of them still wrangled about who had asked who to marry whom. Marnie sensed that this might become an on-going joke between them, never settled. But who would marry them, when, and where, were real questions.

The one thing they agreed on was they would not get married in Israel. And they would use one of the new egalitarian *Ketubot.* In that way, symbolically, and for them in reality, neither of them would be bound to the other in a powerless role.

Neither of them would willingly commit to the system in Israel. "It's kind of awful, both of us being rabbis, but it has too many bad associations. Let's keep it American," was how Marnie put it. With that decided there were a lot of other choices to think about.

"You're the bride, Marnie. You get to pick. That's the quick answer. You get to pick the dress, the flowers, the place, the meal, the music, the rabbi, the photographer, the whole thing. You've already picked the groom. That's the important part, don't you think?"

"Of course. But that wasn't a problem, just a surprise. How do you know all this, anyway?"

"All those brothers of mine mean I have all those sisters-in-laws. Believe me, they all got to pick. My mother learned to put up with it until she got to marry off my sisters. Then it was her turn. In this case, my parents will so pleased I'm finally getting married, they won't mind one bit."

"If I get to pick, then I'd like Tovah to marry us," Marnie said. "At her synagogue in Dana Point. How do you feel about that?"

Tovah was Marnie's best friend. She had humored Marnie all those years, even when she knew Marnie was keeping secrets. And, she had helped Eli navigate through the first days of getting to know Marnie.

"Tovah would have been my choice," Eli said.

"To get back to our parents. We should tell them, you know." Marnie worried. Neither set of parents had been officially informed.

"We just decided two days ago. We'll do it soon. Let's figure a few things out. Like where and when."

The issue of when led them to the calendar. It was already October and they didn't want to wait very long. They would be married within the next few months.

1997 was one of those rare years when Christmas and Chanukah coincided, Marnie reported, really delighted. Late December would be the perfect time. She checked the voluminous *luach,* the Jewish calendar that contained the dates of the Jewish year relative to the regular calendar.

"This year the holidays are on our side," Eli said. "Perfect. We get married in California, sometime between December 23, the first night of Chanukah, and January 3. My birthday is the fourth night of Chanukah. That'll be Tuesday, December 27 this year. I'll be 37. We could do it then. Would you like that?"

Marnie liked that idea very much. In fact, it gave her a wonderful idea for a wedding gift, one they would actually share, a custom made *Ketubah,* a real art piece, with the fourth night of Chanukah as its theme. She didn't quite know how to manage such a gift. She would need some help.

Eli didn't seem to notice her momentary distraction. His plans for their wedding was already full blown in his mind.

"You know, *Yeshivot* don't like to acknowledge they pay attention to Christmas and the secular new year, but this year when they break for Chanukah it will also mean they'll be closed for Christmas. They won't start school until the first Monday after the New Year.

He took the calendar out of Marnie's hands. "Look. First Monday after the New Year is January 5, 1998. Perfect! Your university will be closed for the winter holiday, at the same time. No conflict. Pluperfect!! Even if there are other weddings or *b'nai mitzvot* planned for December at Tovah's synagogue, they're unlikely to be on a Tuesday. Plus, because it's vacation time, most people will be able to travel."

"People?"

Sometimes one word was all Marnie could manage in the face of Eli's enthusiasms. "People. Yours from New York and Santa Barbara. Mine from New York, Philly, Dallas, you know. From everywhere. And Israel, too." Eli smiled at Liora.

Liora grinned back. "I'll be there," she promised.

"Everyone will come. From everywhere."

"Everyone?" Marnie managed to repeat.

"We'll confirm with Tovah when she gets back from the dig, and then we'll call your folks and my folks. Tell my father, call my mother. She won't like to hear it over the phone, but I couldn't get her to come to Israel this time. She was just here when we bought the *Yeshiva* building. She says she's getting to old to travel so far. Just watch her travel when we have kids. She'll come to the ends of the earth if necessary."

"Kids?"

"We agreed we'd like to have kids, right?"

"I'll baby sit," Liora offered. "Anytime."

"Kids," Marnie said, smiling hugely.

Why worry about the details, as Eli said. Marnie never thought she'd take that attitude toward details, but she seemed to be able to do it now. She'd thought she'd never have children of her own. Now she had Liora back, and they were planning for 'kids.' She made a promise to herself, not one she'd even shared with Eli yet. They were going to have a big family, at least four, all of them born before she turned forty.

Later, when Liora had gone to work at her *gan*, they went back to the details.

The major thing was that they would ask Tovah the minute she got back from the dig.

✡

When they were not together, Eli stayed in his own apartment, going to work every morning, jotting down new musical ideas in the afternoon. He joined Marnie and Liora for outings in the late afternoon. When the girl didn't have to work, they played tourist. They visited David's tunnel under the city, shopped in the *shuq* and saw a few other sites. Liora and Marnie continued to share the hotel room that usually housed Tovah and Marnie.

Marnie's time alone with Eli was precious. They were still exercising the restraint the small Fiat and the hammock had helped them with, but it was getting much harder. Fortunately they only had the time when Liora was at work, or after she had gone to bed. Marnie was unwilling to leave the girl alone for hours and hours.

Marnie tackled the issue of her jobs by sending letters to the heads of her departments at the university and the *yeshiva*, in L.A. She promised to complete her teaching for the rest of the current semester, while telling them she would be renegotiating her contracts after that. For several terms, she would be looking for a generous leave of absence and research time.

One morning, after she returned from the north, Marnie took Liora on a shopping spree. Shopping in the stores that stocked the modest clothing women the orthodox community favored, both came away with new wardrobes, a couple of striking dresses, skirts and blouses in wonderfully cool fabrics that flowed around them, giving Liora especially the look of a fairy-tale princess.

The 'girls,' which was what the sales ladies in the stores had called them, and which Marnie rather enjoyed hearing, both now owned two fancy at-home robes, usually known as '*Shabbes* robes'. These were fairly elaborate, loose garments women wore on Friday night for Sabbath dinners.

At dinner after their shopping trip, Marnie said to Eli, "I don't think there's been anything as elegant on the market since the tea gowns of the 1920's and 30's. You should see them. Mine is white with gold and silver trim down the front and…"

Liora interrupted her. "Don't tell him about mine. I'll wear it this week for Shabbat dinner at the hotel and he'll see." She actually smiled at Eli.

Now Liora seemed to be quite willing to cede Eli to Marnie and to enjoy the wedding details. It was almost as though she treated them like parents. Well, maybe more like an aunt and uncle bent on spoiling her. Either way, Liora no longer outlined the words 'he' or 'him' with barbed wire when she spoke about Eli. Often she simply called him by name. In public, Marnie noticed that he'd become, "Rabbi Adler."

At the same dinner, after their shopping trip, they had just been served mint tea when Marnie got a phone call from Tovah.

"It's been raining at the dig since we left," she reported after the call.

"And more is expected tomorrow, so they're on their way home early. They'll be here by nine tonight."

"Let's go meet them," Liora suggested. "People always like to be met. You like it." Marnie and Eli agreed. Liora waiting for them in front of the King David had made for a nice home-coming.

The three of them treated themselves to one of the luscious shredded pastry Arabic desserts that looked like a bird's nest filled with whole candied pistachio 'eggs'. The confection was tinted in delicate pinks and greens and doused in honey syrup. They had more mint tea with it.

"Can you find this in Orange County?" Liora wanted to know. "As dessert for the wedding dinner?"

She and Eli smiled at each other. When they had been shopping, Marnie told him, it was Liora who had insisted they look at wedding dresses.

They had finished dinner and were walking up to the hotel when the bus arrived. It was heavily streaked with mud from the dig, and additional layers of dust picked up as they'd passed through the lowlands. As it pulled in, it was forced to share the space with two other vehicles arriving at the same moment.

There was a somewhat battered *sherut*, a low-cost, multi-person cab, and an elegant white limousine, both arriving from the airport.

Bellhops poured out of the revolving front hotel doors, guiding their large brass luggage racks so they could take care of all of the paraphernalia of their passengers from the bus, limo and the *sherut*.

All the doors of all the vehicles opened at once. Several of the limo doors, most of the six doors of the sherut and the two doors, front and back, of the bus simultaneously clipped parts of other vehicles or crashed into at least one other vehicle or another door as they opened. The din – metal on metal, scratch, bang, scrape, echo and re-echo – sounded like a major traffic accident, although there were no bodies strewn around.

In addition, the luggage wells on both sides of the bus popped open with unholy screeches. At the same moment Tovah and all the class members poured out of the bus and clustered around trying to find their baggage.

As the doors of bus, *sherut* and limo slammed into each other and into the sides of other vehicles, several passengers and the *sherut* driver left their vehicles. Passengers, who couldn't get out, opened their windows and began berating each other in vibrant Hebrew.

"Okay, this is chaos," Eli said laughing. "I've never seen anything like this."

"And you probably never will again," Marnie agreed, also amused at the din and confusion.

"A *balagan*," Liora said, using the perfect Hebrew word for chaos.

Since the bus held so many, Tovah's class won the battle for ground space, grabbing their luggage and responding to the verbal abuse heaped on them in fine style.

Several days in Israel meant the whole class had honed their everyday Hebrew, especially the casual phrases needed for this kind of confrontation. Without paying much attention to the blockage they were creating, they hunted for, and then hauled out their sleeping bags, back backs and duffle bags, everything they had packed for the trip to the dig, plus the boxes and bags of things they had purchased in Tiberius and at other spots on their trip.

Perhaps it was unfortunate that these rabbis, usually somewhat dignified, no longer resembled tidy tourists or sophisticated travelers.

What they resembled most was a group of very dirty children returning from summer camp. Everyone who'd been on the bus was mud stained, bedraggled, and badly in need of showers and shampoos, not to mention clean clothes.

The driver of the limousine, especially, saw no reason to be polite to these ragamuffins, who in his mind, did not belong at the King David. As the driver of a high-priced limousine, and also a high-paid driver and an official guide, he thought that these lowlifes must belong at the YMCA located just across the way. Obviously, they were only squatting at the King David.

The *YimKah*, as the Y was known in Israel, often hosted groups that really belonged, in the drivers mind, in youth hostels or even lower-class accommodations.

The driver's method of attempting to clear the blockage under the portico of the hotel was to blast his horn at the group adding his rude suggestions as to where this dirty group ought to go. Certainly, they should stop sullying the hotel his clients had selected.

The group, still rifling through the bus's luggage wells, totally ignored him during the first and second volleys from his horn. Equally, they paid no attention to what he was screaming at them. Finally, though, Tovah turned around, slung a back pack and duffle over her shoulder, freeing her hands, and gave him the finger. This shocked Liora, who, although she had once done the same to Eli, could not believe that Tovah or Marnie knew the sign or what it meant.

Like most drivers and guides, this one had advanced security training and was probably a *Krav Maga* – Israel Martial Arts – specialist. He slammed out of his seat to give this insulting young woman a lecture. He was stopped by one of his passengers.

"Urik," an American voice said. "Don't! She's a rabbi. They're all rabbis. They'll all look better when they're cleaned up."

Urik only stopped because his obviously wealthy American client had given him a direct order, not because he believed him. In the meantime, though, he went back to blowing his horn. He also shoved open his door again, just in case he had to leave his car to defend his obviously crazy client. His door slammed up against the bus with a resounding crack, adding to the din.

If not for his American passenger's direct order, the driver would have personally taught the young woman with curly hair a lesson in manners, Israeli style.

The client's voice had effectively cut through the noise of the horn and the driver's outrage so Marnie knew exactly who had said those words: her father.

There, standing at one of the open doors of the limo, were her parents, looking as elegant as ever, as though they were about to host one of their famous casual parties on their ocean-side patio.

"Daddy!" was all Marnie could manage. Without missing a beat, her father, looking perfect, even after traveling a total of twenty hours from California to Jerusalem, waved at her. His gesture said, 'Just give me a minute, while I get this all straightened out.' He would have made Fred Astaire proud.

Walter and Beatrice Holland looked like advertise-ments for the good life in California. Bea wore flower-printed sportswear: lounge pants, an elegant peasant-style top and a filmy matching jacket. Her father, as usual, had found the most elegant sweat-suit in the world, navy blue, the zippered jacket layered over a white silk t-shirt.

Her mother's make up was perfect and her father had obviously taken the trouble to shave in the tiny, on-board first class bathroom.

Even if their appearance in Israel was a total surprise, Marnie realized they were just who she needed to help plan a wedding, to assist her, Liora and Tovah, in buying a wedding dress, and also to get her special gift for Eli underway. Trust her parents to show up exactly when and where they were needed.

Marnie was just thinking about how to get to them, how to brave the traffic jam under the portico of the hotel, when another woman got out of the limo after her parents. She was tall, thin and had once-red hair now graying to a shade of apricot.

Suddenly, beside her, Eli started waving and laughing.

"Hi, Mom," he called across the chaos of cars, lug-gage, busses, a cab and the limo.

"These are the wonderful people I traveled with from New York. I understand we have a lot in common," the woman said, loud enough to be heard.

She had to be Eli's mother; the height, the hair, mak-ing that very clear.

She put one hand on each of the shoulders of Marnie's mother and father.

Eli hopped up on one of the brass luggage carts, skated it over to the edge of the driveway, and, using it as a jumping off point, launched himself from the roof of the *sherut* which had by now maneuvered up to the curb, totally cutting off the limo.

Eli vaulted over the *sherut's* hood and landed lightly near the limo's rear end. There, he first hugged his mother and was then introduced by her to Marnie's parents.

Marnie had to wait until all this was accomplished. She knew she couldn't possibly follow Eli in his high jump over the vehicles, so she had to watch. After introductions, the four of them turned and waved to her and Liora. Marnie wished she had a camera.

Beside her, Liora was laughing in a way Marnie had never heard from the girl before.

Then, suddenly, Liora stopped laughing. She went so silent so quickly that Marnie turned from the scene of her parents, a potential in-law and her fiancée getting to know each other eight unreachable feet away to look at the girl.

Liora was standing beside her, pointing to the rear of the *sherut*. Shalom was exiting from a rear door of the cab that had once been some sort of stretch Mercedes. Shalom turned and guided a young girl out, but without touching her. Once he'd cleared the way for the girl by pushing aside the vehicle's door, he reached in and pulled out two carry-on El Al airline bags and then set to work moving toward the rear of the *sherut*, probably to retrieve the rest of their luggage.

Liora had gone white, although Marnie didn't think Shalom had seen either one of them yet. She doubted Shalom was staying at the King David, but his fiancée might be, if her parents had approved her trip to Israel.

Beside her she felt Liora tremble and she sensed the girl was about to turn and run back into the hotel, attempting to disappear.

"Oh, no," she said. "We stand right here. We haven't done one thing wrong. We've got every right to be together here. You'd have been alone otherwise. Eli and I will talk to your father if we have to."

Liora swallowed once, then again, clearly she was seeking for a brave front she could assume. She grabbed Marnie's hand for physical and moral support. Then, surprisingly, she laughed again and pointed once more. There was an addition to the driveway. It didn't seem possible. Added to the dirt-streaked bus, the *sherut* and the long, white limo was a small truck, with one blue door and one red door. Sammy was driving, and had tucked his van into the miniscule space the *sherut* had created when it edged over to the curb. It was going to take the door man a while to untangle the people, luggage and vehicles in the driveway.

Usually the staff could almost magically sweep any confusion from the front of the hotel and into the lobby where the elegant desk staff quickly sorted them into their correct rooms, suites, pool-side accommodations or bungalows. Right now, however, no one was moving.

Sammy, arriving in the Gasith-family vehicle, adding to the confusion, was a wonderful touch. Clearly he was there to pick up the bridal couple.

Whether this represented a real rapprochement between father and son, or was just a momentary accommodation, Marnie didn't know. As she watched, Sammy, standing on the edge of the crowd, pulled out a small camera and began snapping pictures of the crowd. He probably knew some paparazzo, some publication, or even one of the new websites, where he could make a dollar or two with pictures like this. Minimally, he'd have a picture for his own website of the kind of confusion his services allowed his clients to avoid.

When Shalom saw Marnie and Liora standing together, he herded his fiancée over to his son, who shoehorned the girl into the truck. Then much to Marnie's surprise Shalom walked away, to complete some business she supposed.

Sammy drove off with Katie. Marnie remembered one of the first things Liora had reported. What Sammy had said about Shalom being too old to marry Katie, or Katie being too young. And that Sammy liked Katie, "maybe too much." Marnie wondered if leaving Katie and Sammy alone was such a good idea.

Well, there was nothing she could do about it, nothing she could say to Shalom. Shalom very pointedly snubbed her completely. Clearly, she would never get to talk to Katie. Shalom also shook his finger at his daughter before he walked away.

Liora had teared up over that, as any daughter would. Marnie put her arm tightly around the girl, promising that her *Abba* was probably more upset now then he would be later.

She was able to distract Liora by saying, "look, here come my parents. They've left Eli to deal with the luggage and they want to hug us. As far as my parents are concerned they just got their granddaughter back."

Marnie's parents had worked their way free of the crowd and were bearing down of them. Eli's mother was right behind them.

Liora might have objected, not a hundred percent certain she should allow Walter to touch her, but she was powerless when the two older Hollands, after introducing Marnie briefly to Eli's mother, both said, "Liora! Liora! You're all grown up, and so beautiful."

They turned and introduced Liora to Eli's mother. "Raizel. This is Liora. We showed you her pictures from when she was little. Isn't she just as she gorgeous now? Even more so." Then all four of them were hugging.

By now Liora was crying. So were Bea Holland and Raizel Adler. Walter had the smile Marnie had only seen when her father was especially proud of her.

What a gift! Her parents could so easily include Liora back into the family. How could she ever be angry with her father, despite his meddling over her original wedding? All he'd done was try to save her from herself.

"I'll explain it all to them later," Liora whispered to Marnie. "About not touching and all that. It isn't right to hurt their feelings, not now. Not ever. Did you know they still have picture of me?"

"We all do," Marnie said.

For Marnie and Eli, all the people they needed to plan their wedding were at hand. Their two-month-calendar had moved into its final phase.

AFTERWORD

Two years later
July, 1999

Los Angeles, California

As much as Rabbi Marnie Adler – she had changed her last name when she married Eli, much to her friends amazement – had traveled in less than two years, the Los Angeles airport always brought back a flood of memories.

There had been her flight home when she escaped her first husband, Shalom. She had thought she would never be able to go back to Israel, never be able to live anywhere near Shalom again, always too afraid. And she was certain her step-children were lost to her forever.

Then had come the trip back for her first year of rabbinical school. She had known no one, and she still feared Shalom, but the school required it. So, she worked with her parents to create a kind of disguise. She no

longer wore the wig or other head-covering of an orthodox woman. She'd cropped her blonde hair short, and
lightened it. Contact lenses had replaced her glasses. In
addition, she wore jeans and t-shirts, carried a backpack
and told her parents she planned to stay in the dorm
throughout the year. Except when her parents visited,
or when the school required it, she'd stuck to her plan.

Then, just two years ago, Shalom had arrived in
Los Angeles, making what seemed like an outrageous
demand. Marnie had maneuvered her friend Tovah into
letting her join their class reunion in Israel, a trip she'd
sworn she'd never make.

How her life had changed! All her secrets had been
destroyed. Her new life had begun.

Her later, wonderful, memories were what she would
focus on now. Except, she didn't have a minute.

"Whoever said there are only two types of travel – first
class and with children–was right," Eli said, contemplating
the pile of suitcases and baby equipment just liberated
from the El Al luggage carousel at LAX.

"S.J. Perelman," Marnie said.

She was doing her best to hang on to her small son.
He was doing his best to get away. At least she didn't
have to worry about Mia, her new baby, because Liora
Gasith stood nearby, cradling her.

"Well, as always, it's peaceful, compared to the total
confusion that day when everyone arrived in Israel at
the same moment," Eli said.

That day remained their measure of utter chaos.
Anything less could always be managed.

"Liora, you should sit down. Mia might be small, but you've been holding her for a long time," Marnie said to her step-daughter, who was checking the baby for the umpteenth time.

Mia, Eli and Marnie's new baby, not quite three months old, was sleeping. It was hard to believe, given passengers from three international flights were disembarking around them, but the Adlers had already learned their youngest was like that. She kept to her schedule. The adults might not know what time it was in Israel, but the baby knew it was either night time or nap time. She slept.

"No place to sit," the teenager said, not looking very concerned.

"Sit there," Marnie said, indicating the edge of the luggage carousel, now stationary.

Liora sat. With two of her charges looked after, Marnie tried to concentrate on Ezra, but her son managed to escape.

"Get him," she said desperately to her husband. Eli might be tired, but he had long legs. In two strides he captured his 16-month old son.

The adults waited for the explosions of 'don' wanna, don' wanna, no, no, no,' from Ezra, in English and Hebrew, but Eli staved that off by swinging his son up to sit on his shoulders.

"Going up," Eli said, and the little boy subsided immediately. Sitting on the shoulders of his six-foot four father was second best to running free in what seemed the limitless space of the international terminal. Fortunately it was a close second. Ezra buried one fist in his father's red hair, the same color as his own, and then greeted the world around him, waving his free hand

and crowing, "Shalom, Shalom." A surprising number of travelers happily responded to him.

Liora, always practical, and tranquil, said, "Dan will be here for us soon."

"He will," Marnie confirmed. "He said to wait here. Not to try to get to the curb."

At that moment Eli joined Ezra in waving. He'd spotted Dan and the bar mitzvah boy, Ari, loping toward them. They were coming to California to celebrate Ari's bar mitzvah at Tovah's synagogue, Ohel Tikvah, in Dana Point. Eli and Marnie had been married there in December of 1997.

Tovah Feldner stood in the hallway of her Dana Point home. "Everything is under control," she said to Marnie, who had finished nursing Mia and was now carrying her into the living room where Eli was reading *Goodnight Moon* to Ezra.

"Would you have it any other way?" Marnie said.

The two women, with the baby on a blanket between them, curled up on the couch.

Liora was sitting in a far corner of the room working on a laptop computer.

"Homework," she said. "The *Rosh* of my high school gets very upset if I don't get my work done, no matter where we are. I try to do it the same day he sends it. Sometimes the time difference works in my favor, sometimes not."

"*Goodnight Moon* is always in English?" Tovah asked, watching Eli with his son.

"No. The moon is bilingual. One night it's in English, one night in Hebrew. I'm not sure he knows there are actually two languages. But, he always turns the pages in the right direction. Who knows what a kid is thinking."

"He won't demand French lessons at four?" Tovah said.

"God forbid," Eli said. "With the children I pray for her looks and my I.Q. You know, high enough to be useful; not high enough to be scary."

"It didn't scare you," Tovah said.

"Of course it scared me," Eli said. "But from the minute I saw her on the security camera at the front door of my *Yeshiva*, I was working the 'never let her see you sweat,' method."

"I guess it worked," Marnie commented.

Tovah had to marvel at Marnie, sitting relaxed, a state previously unknown to her, and making jokes, a skill no one ever knew Marnie possessed.

"I'm done," Liora said, closing the lid of the lap top and disconnecting it. "You've got great computer speed here. Let me take Mia and put her down for the night. She's in your room, right? And *Reb* Eli, when you and Ezra are done, if you'll bring him to our room, the two of us will go to sleep. I'm beat."

Eli nodded and continued reciting the book. Quite suddenly the little boy put his thumb in his mouth, leaned back against his father's chest and closed his eyes. "Down for the count," Eli said, and he picked up Ezra and followed Liora down the hall.

The two women watched him go. "He's a good guy," Tovah said.

"Very good," Marnie agreed. "I mean look at all he's accomplished in just over two years."

"He's accomplished? What about you? You had nothing to do with it?

Just then Marnie got up suddenly. "Oh my goodness," she said. "I have to tell Eli something before he goes to sleep."

All Tovah heard was a couple of muffled sentences in the hall and then a whoop of laughter from Eli, and a loud 'shhhhh' sound from Marnie.

She was back in under a minute, laughing.

"What's the joke?" Tovah asked.

"Jokes on me," Marnie said. "I gave Eli the wrong quote in the airport. You know: There are two ways to travel in America, first class and with children. I didn't have all of it and I told him it was S.J. Perleman."

Tovah looked confused. "And that was important, because…."

"It was wrong," Marnie said, with a momentary return of something like her old rigor. She was laughing at herself, too.

"First of all, it was Robert Benchley who actually said it." Marnie ticked off her first point on her finger.

"Second, it applied so beautifully at that moment. You had to be there. And…"

By now Tovah was laughing with her friend and at her too. "Is there really a third point?"

Marnie looked at her fingers where she was ticking of her points. "Well, I had to tell him I'd been wrong."

It was Tovah's turn. "You know Marnie. It's good to know someone can change so much, but still stay the same, fundamentally. It's reassuring. Two kids in two years, living in Israel, married of course, even with a new name. Commuting to teach Talmud and helping with Eli's music. But you haven't changed."

"Is that good or bad?" Marnie said

"I'm trying to tell you that I love you and the way you are. I'm trying to tell you that you found a great sense of humor and a sense of relaxation somewhere. I hope whatever you had to give up was worth it."

"I only had to give up my secrets," Marnie said. "That left lots of room for life."

The End

TOPICS FOR BOOK CLUBS TO PONDER

Over the last couple of years I have joined and left a couple of new books clubs. Once again I find the 'find a list of questions and ask them one after another' method, less useful then a more freewheeling discussion. But, I love book clubs and I know having some idea of what the author had in mind is useful and provides jumping off points.

Did the title of this book, *An Unorthodox Romance,* and the cover art draw your interest? Or is the idea of a relatively young woman having a chance to restart her life and correct a past mistake more intriguing?

Judaism and its many divisions is a major topic in *An Unorthodox Romance.* Do you think the divisions – Reform, Conservative, Orthodox – are similar to division in other religions. For example in Christianity – Methodist, Presbyterian, Anglican, or Unitarian – or are the distinctions between Catholic and Protestant more similar. Also in Islam, the various main groups: Sunni and Shia?

This is the third of a trilogy of interlocking books. Do you enjoy books where characters come and go, sometimes featured and sometimes in the background? I asked the same question in my other two novels: *The Binding* and *The Rabbi's Husband*.

Before you read this book did you have a fairly good knowledge of Judaism, Torah and Talmud, or were these new to you? Do you think all people of faith would enjoy reading *An Unorthodox Romance?*

www.ingramcontent.com/pod-product-compliance
Lightning Source LLC
Chambersburg PA
CBHW060528260626
47161CB00003B/810